PANDEMONIUM ROAD

THOMAS EMSON

snowbooks

Proudly Published by Snowbooks in 2011

Copyright © 2011 Thomas Emson

Thomas Emson asserts the moral right to
be identified as the author of this work.
All rights reserved.

Snowbooks Ltd
email: info@snowbooks.com
www.snowbooks.com

British Library Cataloguing in Publication Data
A catalogue record for this book is available from the British
Library.

ISBN 978-1-906727-33-8

PANDEMONIUM
ROAD

THOMAS EMSON

WHEN THE DEVIL'S ON YOUR TAIL
YOU'D BETTER DRIVE LIKE HELL

CHAPTER 1.
EXECUTION.

THE man with wings cut off my father's head. My heart nearly stopped. I wanted to run out of the shed and try to save my dad.

But it was too late.

He was dead.

He'd been executed by the angel of death.

For a while, they had been talking. Dad and the angel. Gesticulating as if they were discussing who had the biggest carrots. But then the angel swiped his wing across the front of my father's throat. If he had been trying to hit my dad, it looked at first like he'd missed.

But he hadn't.

My dad's mouth opened, and his eyes gaped. His head tilted back – and kept tilting back till it fell off his shoulders and landed at his feet.

His body sagged, and he hit the ground.

His blood was on the grass and in the soil, and his head lay in the vegetable patch he'd cultivated for years.

My dad would spend most of his time at the allotment. Since Mum had died, he felt lonely in the house. And because I was never there, he thought it was pointless staying in.

So he'd come tend his vegetables and chat to his mates.

I knew the place quite well, because I hid here sometimes when the police were after me. Hunkering down in Dad's shed, I'd feel strangely close to him. His tools were there – the spade, the rake, the hoe. A wheelbarrow rested against the wall on its handles. A watering can was tucked in the corner. Sacks of fertilizer were piled at the far end. Packets of seeds littered a table, alongside my father's gardening gloves.

It was his place. It was him.

We never said much to each other. I never felt that close to him. He always eyed me suspiciously. But I was a handful.

My parents would argue over me.

Mum would defend me. "They've made a mistake – it wasn't my Jimmy."

Dad would say, "We have to nip it in the bud, Sonya, or when he's older, we'll have a problem on our hands – a six-foot, twelve-stone, big-lad-shaped problem."

I never got to six foot. Five-eight. Ten-and-a-half stone. Not a hefty teenager, but still a big problem.

Whatever Dad used to say to Mum back when I was a kid, it was always he who covered for me when I did get into trouble.

He'd tell the Old Bill I was somewhere else when they said I was behind the wheel of a taken-without-the-owner's-consent BMW doing a ton down the A2.

He covered for me all the time.

When the police came round he'd say, "He's not here," while I'd be cowering in my bedroom.

When the teachers rang to ask why I wasn't at school he'd say, "He's sick today," while I was playing truant with Tyler.

And when the man with wings came looking for me, he did the same.

He protected me.

He told me to stay out of the way and find somewhere to hide.

He'd said, "Son, you stay in this shed and keep yourself out of sight – and whatever you see or hear, do not come out."

So I was stowed away in the shed among his things, the smell of the soil on those tools the same as the smell of my father.

He was the soil, he was the earth.

He was my dad.

And he was dead.

Shock had frozen me to the spot. Only the top of my head and my eyes were visible as I peered out of the dust-covered window.

The winged man stood over my father's corpse, silhouetted against the sun as it dropped behind the horizon.

I started to shake.

Tears burned my eyes. I tried to blink them away, but it only made them flow.

My vision blurred for a moment, and when it cleared again I saw the angel slowly turning his head towards the shed – towards me.

And then he was looking straight at me.

My blood felt icy.

He knew where I was.

He'd seen me.

And he ran straight towards the shed with his big, black wings spread out behind him, flapping against the twilight.

CHAPTER 2.
LAST CHANCE.

CANTERBURY MAGISTRATES COURT,
BROAD STREET – 11.14AM, JUNE 3, 2011

"YOU'VE had many opportunities, Mr Chance," the magistrates' chairman had said that morning. He was a rat-faced fella and glared at me over his half-moon specs. "I'm not sure you deserve another one."

"I do, your honour," I said.

"Be quiet, Mr Chance," said Rat-Face. I knew him. Not his name, his face. From where I was standing, I'd seen him quite often. My brief touched my arm and smiled, but his eyes were telling me to shut up.

"You are seventeen, Mr Chance," said Rat-Face. "It is time you grew up. Perhaps you should consider your future. Do you have any ambitions?"

I said nothing, playing it dumb – I'd been told to shut up, so I was keeping it shut.

The magistrate sighed. "You may speak."

"Cheers, your honour – "

"I am not 'your honour'. I am 'your worship'."

"Cheers, your worship."

"You should know by now how to address me, Mr Chance – you've been here often enough."

That was true, and I did know. I was just playing the fool.

"Now," said Rat-Face, "your future, young man."

"I'd like to be a racing driver, your worship."

He raised his eyebrows. "Would you? I see. Well, stealing cars and driving them at ridiculous speeds down the A2 and refusing to stop for police are not good preparations for such a career."

"I'd argue it was, your worship."

My brief nudged me.

Rat-Face went crimson. His buddies on the bench bristled. One was a toad-like creature with a comb-over. The other, a woman, looked like a praying mantis. I think the females eat the males. She looked like she could wolf me down. She had steel-grey hair and unblinking eyes. Her mouth was always set in a frown. It had never smiled in all the years I'd seen her at court.

Ratty said, "Perhaps if you showed this court some respect, Chance, you would not be tempted to steal other people's property."

"I doubt that, sir – aw!"

My brief had kicked me in the ankle. It hurt. I had to sit to rub it.

"Are you all right, Mr Chance?" said Ratty.

Before I could say anything my brief stood up.

"Your worships," he said. "James Chance is not a common thug. In fact he is an intelligent young man. Often among the brightest of students at his former schools. But he does have a mouth on him."

"He is gobby, Mr Anwar," said Rat-Face.

A ripple of laughter went through the courtroom. I chuckled too, eager to please. You laugh at people's jokes, they like you a little better. Maybe Rat-Face would warm to me and go easy on me over this taking-without-consent charge.

You've got to hope.

Still smiling, I looked around the court to see if everyone was happy. They were. I felt it was going to be okay.

10

But then I saw her.

She was sitting at the back, arms folded. She gave me a cold, hard stare. It seemed to go all the way through my chest into my spine.

I found it easier to stare at the three magistrates and their unpleasant mugs than look at her beautiful face.

A sweat broke out on my back.

Her eyes still bored into me, making me feel guilty.

The Old Bill could accuse me all day. The beaks on the bench too. And all the teachers who ever shouted at me over the years. I cared nothing for them. Their indictments meant nothing.

But now, in those eyes, I realize I'd been accused by an angel.

My angel.

And I wasn't sure I could get away with it.

CHAPTER 3.
MY ANGEL.

SHE was sitting on a wall outside the court, waiting for me.

She wasn't happy. Her arms were folded, like they'd been inside, and her foot was going up and down.

I was sweating with nerves.

Dealing with magistrates, police, and lawyers was easy compared to dealing with Samantha Louise Rayer.

Sammie.

My Sammie.

The court gave me probation – again. And a community punishment – again.

It would involve cleaning graffiti off bus shelters and sweeping up litter. A doddle. But punishment was always a piss-take. They never sent you down. No room in jail. And what they call "low-level" criminals, like me, should be sentenced using "other methods".

If they sent me down, I'd probably become a hardened criminal.

I don't read papers or anything, but kids talk. You can get the truth on Facebook. You very quickly get to learn what you can and can't do, and if there's any changes in the law.

Truth is, if you were on the ball, then crime paid.

It was a laugh.

And you were never properly penalized.

Not till you met an angel, that is.

My angel.

I walked towards her, bricking myself.

"Hi, babe," I said.

She never looked at me. Kept her eyes fixed on Broad Street. On the city walls across the street.

I looked at her long, blonde hair and remembered how like silk it was to touch and how lovely it was to smell. A yearning came to my heart, but it was mingled with guilt.

"You let me down," she said without turning.

Sammie was sixteen. She was delicate and deadly. A five-foot-tall whirlwind. Slim like a model and as tough as leather. She was like a doll, and she'd been my girlfriend for two years. I wanted no one else.

Why would I? She was gorgeous.

I never understood my mates. Some of them had girlfriends but cheated on them.

The guys said, "It's just the way – blokes get off with birds and birds expect it."

But not me. I didn't want anyone except Sammie. She made me feel tingly all over. When I was with her, everything was calm. I was never tempted to steal or get pissed. I felt something special for her and wasn't embarrassed to admit it.

I was in love.

She turned round, and her eyes were full of tears. It broke my heart.

She said, "You promised me."

I had promised. More than once. But I'd broken them all.

"Never again, Sammie," I said. "Honest, now. I'll go to college. We'll get a flat together. I love you, babe. I really do."

"I don't think I can be with you any more, Jimmy."

My legs weakened. I had a dizzy spell. A great hole felt like it had opened up in my chest, and my heart dropped into it.

"It wasn't my fault," I said, the stock excuse.

And she knew it.

"Are you serious, Jimmy?"

My mouth opened but no words came out – no crap, no lies, no excuses.

I shut my gob and shook my head before saying, "I'm sorry, Sammie."

She looked away, and she trembled.

"Don't cry," I said. "Please, babe."

"You hurt me, Jimmy."

Her words sliced through me. But I'd heard them before. They always hurt, but I always healed.

And after healing, I'd break her heart again.

She turned to me, her eyes red with tears. It made me flinch to see her pain.

She said, "It's over, Jimmy. I have to finish with you."

I flushed, panic racing through me.

I'd never heard these words before. Not even as a threat. They were devastating. You could've told me I was going inside for ten years, and I would've coped with it better.

"It's over," she said.

She burst into tears and ran off down the road.

I started chasing after her, desperate to salvage our relationship. How would I cope without Sammie? She was everything to me. The glue that held me together.

I was ready to run after her, but a piercing whistle stopped me in my tracks. I wheeled round, saw who had whistled, and sighed.

"You're the last person I need to see," I said.

CHAPTER 4.
WHO NEEDS MATES?

"HERE," said Tyler Jackson, "that's no way to talk to your best mate."

"Best mates don't run off and leave you. Best mates don't disappear and let you take the fall. Best mates back you up."

I walked away from him. I didn't want to be near Tyler or the court. I wanted to be with Sammie and sort out the problem I'd caused.

"And that's what you did," said Tyler. "You backed me up. And I'll never forget that, mate. You're not a grass, and that means something."

He was trotting after me, and I quickened my pace.

I said, "Don't talk crap. You think you're some kind of gangster or something?"

"I know one or two local faces. Does that count?"

"No, it doesn't, Tyler."

"Well, they know me. And you too. We got a reputation, you know."

"Yeah, I know – I'm trying to get rid of it."

"Come on, Jimmy. Here, wait," he said, catching me up. "I got a cracking job for us."

I wheeled and looked him straight in the eyes. "You have got to be joking."

"I never joke. Only with birds."

"And they find you hilarious."

"Sammie likes me."

"You're not reading the signals right, Tyler."

"Come on, it's a great job."

"I said, are you taking the mick? I just got done again, thanks to you. I just got my final warning, Tyler."

"It's always a final warning, mate. You'll be all right. Soft on crime, soft on the causes of crime – you know the law."

"I promised Sammie."

"Didn't do you much good. Last I saw she was legging it down the road. Looked in a bit of a huff to me. She pissed off again? She'll come round. Birds always do."

"Not this time. I'm going round hers. Sort this out. I got to do the right thing, Tyler."

"The right thing is to stick with your mates."

"Just like you did, eh?"

I walked away from him. Tyler had pissed me off. He always pissed me off. We'd been best pals since nursery. He was cheeky and always getting into trouble – always dropping me in it.

I remembered our first encounter. We were four years old.

He stole the nursery teacher's sandwich out of her bag and ate it right in front of the class.

Then he spat out a mouthful of tuna mayo and bread right into my lap.

I gaped at my trousers, covered in crumbs and bits of fish.

"Jimmy Chance," said the high-pitched voice, and I turned to see the teacher standing at the door, scowling at me.

I got the blame, and despite my claims of innocence, there is very little justice in the nursery school system. Circumstantial evidence is enough to condemn you. The burden of proof is not so heavy when you're accusing four year olds of eating your lunch.

So I got told off while Tyler chuckled at the back on the class.

He was a bad influence on me. And sometimes I wondered what kind of mate he was, because he never backed me up. He never stood by me. He was the first to bolt if there was trouble. And he always expected me to take the fall for him.

"That's what mates do," he'd say.

But he'd never do the same for me, despite his pledges of allegiance.

More broken promises, I thought.

But he was a laugh. You were always in stitches with Tyler. You never knew what he would do next. He was unpredictable.

Maybe that was the problem. I needed some stability. I needed Sammie.

As I walked along Broad Street, Tyler shouted after me, "It's a great job. Be fun, Jimmy. Cool car. Mercedes. Come on. You and me, race the cops down the A2. Come on."

Without turning around, I gave him the finger and went to win back my girlfriend.

CHAPTER 5.
SAM'S MUM.

MY head was spinning as I made my way down Military Road.

Court had slipped my mind. My punishment someone else's. Meetings with probation officers could wait.

Those things were nothing. Just a hindrance for a while.

My main concern was Sammie. I just had to get over to hers – and quick. Sort this out. Sort us out. Sort me out.

I was walking home fast. Military Road became the estates off the Sturry Road, where we both lived, just a couple of streets away from each other.

I was sweating, texting as I walked. Texting Sam and asking her to forgive me, please text back, please can we meet.

I was nearly there. My nerves jangled.

Please text back say it's okay, I thought.

My phone beeped. Text. My heart jumped. I checked excitedly. It was from Tyler. I sighed.

He was hassling me: *"Meet at mine. Car Stodmarsh."*

Stodmarsh, I thought, stuffing the phone back in my pocket.

I got to Sammie's house and stopped outside. Toys littered the lawn, her little brother's stuff strewn across the grass.

I felt a pang, remembering him and me playing football in the front garden, Sammie watching and saying, "You're being beaten by a seven year old," and me laughing, letting him win.

I felt gloomy as I went up to the front door and knocked.

The door opened.

My gloom went, and in its place came a cold, nervy feeling. She glared at me, her blue eyes glinting.

Sam's mum. An older version of Sammie. Delicate and deadly, also tough as leather. Very blonde and very beautiful. I had to admit, Sam's mum gave me the hots. It was good to know that in twenty-five years' time, that's what Sammie would look like.

"She doesn't want to see you, Jimmy," she said.

"Could you just tell her I'm here?"

"She knows you're here. That's why she doesn't want to see you."

"What have I done wrong?"

Sam's mum laughed sarcastically. "Are you joking?"

I was going to say it wasn't my fault, but she might have slammed the door in my face. I said nothing instead, my shoulders sagging.

She let out a sigh. "Jimmy, you know I like you. You're a nice boy, and you got brains. Most important, you're good to my Sammie."

I sensed hope and looked at her with my best "give me another chance" look. Her face had softened.

She went on: "But you've made loads of promises – "

"But I – "

"Jimmy, listen to me. You've made loads of promises, I don't know how many – "

"Four – "

"Four, there we are – four. All of them broken. You can't go on like this. Sammie can't go out with a criminal."

"It's over now, I promise."

She pulled a face. "That word again. Promise. Means nothing. Sammie says she doesn't want to see you. It's over. She's very sad about it, Jimmy. But she has made her decision. It's for the best."

"For whose best?"

"For her best."

"I just want her to say it to my face."

"Don't be silly. She's said it to you through me."

"I want her to say it to me, I – "

"It's over, Jimmy," said Sammie's voice from somewhere above me.

I flinched and backed down the path.

She was leaning out of her bedroom window. My heart broke.

Her mum said, "Shut the window and get back inside, Sammie."

I said, "Sammie, listen to me, I – "

Sammie, crying, said, "Jimmy, go away. I can't see you again. I can't. It's… it's breaking my heart. Go away."

She shut the window and was gone.

"Go home, Jimmy," said Sam's mum. "It's over."

She slammed the door in my face.

For a while, I just stood there in Sam's garden with Sam's brother's toys around me. I don't know how long I was there. Seconds or hours. Eventually I trudged away. I looked back once at Sammie's bedroom window. I yearned. I remembered her touch and her smell and the sound of her voice. And losing it all brought tears to my eyes.

CHAPTER 6.
ANOTHER "GOODNIGHT".

WHEN I got home, Dad was sitting in his armchair, watching Coronation Street on ITV2. It was just after lunch, and I could smell beans on toast.

I said, "All right," as I walked in.

Dad said nothing for a minute. He had been at the allotment all morning. He could've come with me to court, but he'd been before and knew how the story ended.

Without looking up at me he said, "You didn't go to jail, then?"

"I did, but I escaped. Me and Charlie Bronson. I'm top of the FBI's most wanted list. Now. Can you hide me in the shed up at the allotment? They'll never think to look up there."

He said nothing, just stared at that bird who used to be in Hear-Say on the telly behind the bar. I stared at her for a bit, too.

Then I said, "Are you going to tell me off?"

"Would it be worth it?"

I sat down on the couch and slung my feet up on the coffee table.

The Corrie ad break came on TV. Cheryl Cole sold shampoo. My dad scratched his chin and sighed. He asked what happened at court.

I told him, and he said, "Same old, same old. D'you get curfew?"

I said yes, and he said, "Same old, same old. Do any good?"

I said yes, and he said, "That'll be the day."

"It's true."

"Seen your Sammie?"

I swallowed, my throat dry.

He looked at me when I didn't answer.

"She's dumped you, hasn't she," said my dad.

I fidgeted with the TV remote control, watching the screen. Red Bus bingo said they sponsored daytime telly on ITV2. Corrie came back for Part Two.

Dad was a bit Mystic Meg-ish in the way that he could suss me out quickly. But maybe it was because I went quiet and my face turned red, and he could probably smell the shame come off me like aftershave.

"Has she dumped you?" he said.

"We had a row."

He shook his head. "Lovely girl. You're an idiot."

"So I'm an idiot for losing Sammie, not for nicking cars, then?"

"Same thing."

I grumbled something.

He said, "Has she dumped you?"

I told him what happened. My dad tutted.

Dad was forty, but he looked sixty. He had grey hair and bags under his eyes. His face was ruddy. That was because he spent so much time outside, the elements affecting his skin. The scotch also helped. He smelled of it now. He'd probably had a tumbler up at the allotment earlier. He never drank in the house. Only in his shed and in the pub.

Forty was old to me, but really it was young. People live anciently these days. But he looked like an old tree, twisted and dry.

It was Mum dying that had made him old.

I was eight at the time, and she'd been ill for a while. I don't remember them ever telling me about her being sick, or that she would die.

She just got sicker and sicker, and he got older and older, till finally she was dead, and he was ancient.

At the time my nan said, "Mum's gone to Jesus, darling."

"Well, Jesus is going to have to give her back," I told her.

"He wants her to be with him, now."

"He's a bastard, then."

"Jimmy, you mustn't say that."

"We've got to rescue her."

"No, darling. She's happy now. She's resting. She's not in pain anymore."

"How do you know, Nan?"

"I… I just know. You've got to have faith, darling."

"Faith?"

"Don't worry, Jimmy. It's going to be okay."

I'm not sure if it was okay. I'm not sure where the line between okay and not okay was. Life just went on.

Dad never talked about it.

Nan tried to but always ended up weeping.

I don't remember crying. I remember dreaming I cried, and the pillow was wet when I woke up. But I'm sure I never actually cried.

After Mum's death, Dad spent more and more time at the allotment and less and less time with me.

When I'd come home from school, Nan was there waiting, and she'd make dinner for me and Dad, trying to talk to us.

Dad grunted. I ate. Nan babbled.

Then we'd watch telly and I'd go to bed. Dad would say, "Goodnight," which was one of the few things he'd say to me all day.

Getting up in the morning, I was nervous and quiet. Dad would be in the kitchen and he'd say, "Morning" and put toast and juice on the table for me and give me my lunch money. When I'd leave for school he'd say, "Be a good boy." And that was it till I got home again to Nan and Dad, and then it was Nan making dinner and telly and another "Goodnight."

Sometimes Dad had to come to school and talk to the headmaster because Tyler had got me into trouble. That was a bit of a change from the old routine, and quite exciting – despite my being in the school's bad books. But Dad never said anything. He never did anything. At the time, when I was eight or nine, I thought he didn't care. But later I realized he cared a lot. He loved me. He just didn't show it.

Like he didn't show it now. He just sat there watching Corrie.

"I'm going out," I said.

He said nothing.

CHAPTER 7.
TROUBLESOME TOYOTA.

UP at the allotment I texted Sammie again. I told her sorry and promised her this time – a real promise. What the other promises were, I don't know. They should've been real too. If I was her, I wouldn't have texted back.

She didn't.

It was quiet at the allotment. It were close to the main road, near the retail park. But it still felt you were in the middle of nowhere.

I could see why Dad came up here.

Thoughts went through my head as I sat on a bench outside my dad's shed. I was still in my suit and I regretted not getting changed. But it wasn't my only regret.

I remembered what my Nan had said about having faith. If I had faith Sammie would get back with me, would it happen? I thought about praying. Maybe God would listen if I really meant it. But I wasn't really sure if there were a God. Such things had never crossed my mind.

I texted her again, and thought about being with her and how it made me feel. Happy, that's how I felt. Safe. Relaxed and excited at the same time.

So why risk all those positive feelings by doing stupid stuff?

The car that had got me into trouble this time was a Toyota.

Well, it wasn't the car. It was Tyler, wasn't it. Always Tyler.

We'd been having a drink in town. I'd had a pint, Tyler a couple. We got kicked out because he got smart and shoved some guy for no reason. The guy slapped him round the ear, and the staff booted us out.

I was pissed off about it, because I was due to meet Sammie there, and we were going to have a night out together.

"You always mess it up," I told him, striding down the road. "She loves that pub, and if we don't get a drink there, she'll be pissed off. Sometimes I think you do it on purpose, keep me from seeing her."

"Ring her, say you're ill," said Tyler.

"I'm not ill, am I."

"So what, just tell her anyway."

"I can't lie to her."

"You're joking, mate."

"I could tell her I'm sick."

"There you go," he said.

"Tell her I'm sick of you. That wouldn't be a lie."

"Come on, Jimmy. The bloke in there was having a go."

"He was doing nothing. And you got slapped for it. Tough. You're just a pain in the arse, Tyler."

"You're not talking like a mate."

"I'm not sure I am one right now."

"Here, look at that," he said.

I stopped and looked. My stomach fizzed. The Toyota sat there with its driver's-side window narrowly open. Just a few inches. Enough. We trotted over to the car, eyes skimming the road. My heartbeat increased. I was getting a sweat on.

The keys were in the ignition.

"Twat," said Tyler. He reached through the open window, stretching his arm inside, and opened he the door. He dived in, but I booted him up the arse, shoving him across from the driver's side to the passenger seat. He complained, saying I always got to drive.

"You've had two pints," I said.

He had argued, but I ignored him, quickly getting into the car and firing up the engine. I rammed it into gear. We were away.

In the rear view mirror, I saw a man lunge out of a house, waving his fist at us, his face red and creased with anger.

Tyler and me laughed as we sped off down the road.

We soon had a copper on our tail. We'd hit the A290, the Whitstable Road, and we sent cars swerving out our way.

The flashing blue lights were soon on our arse.

We laughed our heads off. The adrenaline pulsed. I sweated with excitement. The wheels screeched as I turned left down Forty Acres Road, a residential area. Cops take it slow in residential areas. It can give you the edge.

Pedestrians stopped and pointed. Cars skidded to a halt. It was scary as usual, but still thrilling.

I loved the race. I loved the speed.

My mind was spinning, thoughts of Sammie gone. I buried my guilt at not seeing her. And then I remembered I had to phone her. I lost my concentration.

Tyler shouted something.

I came round to find myself going to quickly into a corner.

A bunch of kids were cycling in the road.

I slammed the brakes.

The smell of burning rubber filled the car.

The tires screeched.

The car bucked and lurched and mounted the kerb.

I was tossed around and clumped my head on the window.

Everything went blurry. I was dizzy.

Tyler screamed. The Toyota went head first into a wall, the impact throwing me forward against the steering wheel.

I must have blacked out for a second, because when I came round, the passenger door was open and Tyler was scampering away, down a side street.

I opened my door, groaning in pain, and fell out of the car, onto the grass.

I opened my eyes and found myself looking at a pair of black boots.

Someone said, "Get up, you git."

Hands grabbed me and lifted me, and I was still dizzy and complaining.

But then the cops were handcuffing me and roughing me up, swearing and shouting, saying I could have killed someone.

"It wasn't me, it wasn't me," I moaned, and when they ignored me, I said, "I'm injured, I'm hurt."

"Stay still, then," one of the Old Bill had said, "or I'll make it hurt some more."

CHAPTER 8.
A CHANGED MAN.

BY the time I headed home from the allotment, which was followed by a stroll around Halfords on the Maybrook Retail Park, it was gone six – it was past my curfew.

But who cared?

No one really kept an eye.

You might get a call from your probation officer now and again checking up on you. But generally you were free to roam.

If you did get picked up by the cops, they might just take you home, or if they were in a bad mood, you'd end up back in court.

But not this time.

I'd learned my lesson.

I was a changed man.

I thought about Sammie all the way home and how I'd make a future for us. I was going to get a job or go back to college. Maybe learn to be a racing driver – and not by pelting around the streets of Canterbury and down the A2.

I walked with determination, ready to tell my dad. Tell him I was changing. Tell him I was growing up. I hope he'd look me in the eye when I told him. I hope that he'd hug me and tell me I was a good lad.

I was up for it – for change, for a new start.

But when I turned the corner into our road, I stopped dead.

It was there outside my house.

The police car.

I loitered at the corner of the street, trying to look as if I was waiting for something or someone.

As I fidgeted with my phone, I looked out of the corner of my eye at the cop car.

They were probably in the house. A pair of them. Always two. I wondered what they were doing, what they were talking about.

Was Dad sat there, watching Judge Judy or Come Dine With Me, two cops drinking tea with him and asking, "Can you tell us where Jimmy could be, Mr Chance?"

Dad wouldn't say. He'd have a good idea where I was, but he wouldn't say. He never said. That was a good thing about Dad. Something I never really appreciated as much as I should have.

I texted Sammie – again.

I tried to ring her – again.

Her phone went to voicemail. It was nice to hear her voice. I shut my eyes and listened. My chest felt warm. Everything became calm. Her voice relaxed me – the little clicks she made when she spoke, the tiny croak because she'd started smoking.

"Leave a message, babes, and I'll get back to you," said her voice.

There was a tone, and then I spoke: "Sammie, it's me. Please ring. The police are outside my house. I don't know what I'm going to do. I'm sorry about everything – "

The phone bleeped. An incoming call. Sammie. I cut off my message. Without checking the caller's ID, I answered and said, "Sammie, I'm really sorry about everything and – "

"Forget Sammie – the car is still there, mate. And they just loaded it with briefcases."

All the energy drained out of me.

It was Tyler.

The last voice I needed to hear.

CHAPTER 9.
NOTHING LEFT.

TYLER said, "It might be cash, mate. It might be jewellery. We can sell it. I know some fellas who'd be interested, and we can – "

"No," I said, interrupting him. "I said no."

"Come on, mate. Come on. Sammie ain't going to come back to you, is she. What's the point hanging on. Do what you do best, Jimmy. Drive. Drive this car. Take it for a spin. Grab what's in the back –"

"What's in the back?"

"I said, briefcases. Thirteen of them."

We sat on the bus as it trundled down the country road headed to the village of Stodmarsh. Tyler was on community punishment at the Stodmarsh National Nature Reserve, picking up litter and drinking tea. He'd spotted the car while in the Probation Service minibus, coming home from a day's rubbish collecting.

I was telling myself now that we were only going to take a look at this Mercedes.

I liked looking at cars and imagining what they'd be like to drive. Imagining what they felt like, my foot flat on the accelerator, my grip on the steering wheel tightening as the speed increased and I battled the car and the road, fighting to stay in control. My arms would ache. The adrenaline would pulse through me.

31

Right, I thought, jazzed by the prospect of the Mercedes, *if Sammie doesn't want me, what's the point?*

My phone rang. It was my dad. I furrowed my brow, not answering, just staring at his number on the ID screen.

Dad never called me. And certainly not using his mobile. He hated the damn thing. He only had a handset in case he ever got stuck anywhere. For a young-ish bloke, he was old.

"Who's that, your bird?" said Tyler.

I said nothing and answered the phone.

"What's wrong, Dad?"

"Is that Jimmy?" said a voice, not my dad.

I said nothing.

The voice said, "Jimmy, if that is you, this is Sergeant Morris from Kent Police, and you know – "

I cut him off.

"Cops," I told Tyler.

He paled. "What's up?"

"I broke my curfew."

"They're keen."

"Court said it was my last chance."

"Always say that."

"Maybe this time they meant it."

"Cops are a pain in the arse. They should leave us alone, man."

In my mind, the future came apart. Not that I had a future. I never thought much about it. I wanted to be a racing driver, but that wasn't going to happen. So instead, I raced cars around the streets. Fast cars. Other people's cars.

And there was also Sammie.

I thought we'd always be together. I was going to sort myself out eventually. It was difficult, that was all. The broken promises would soon all be mended. I would've made it okay in the end.

Probably after this charge… maybe.

But now Sammie had dumped me.

The cops were after me.

I'd be properly punished for failing to stick to my curfew.

No more CPROs. No more cleaning graffiti. No more last chances.

I had nothing.

Nothing except Tyler and this car with thirteen briefcases in the boot.

Thirteen briefcases.

What was inside them?

Cash, maybe.

Lots of cash.

Cash to get me out of Canterbury. Cash to get me out of England.

I could travel to America. Learn to drive Indy 500s.

You need money for everything these days. Nothing's free. Talent counts for nothing. If I could get my hand on some funds, maybe I could get a bit of the everything I'd always wanted.

Thirteen briefcases, I thought. Why not.

CHAPTER 10.
TWOCKING.

THE Mercedes glimmered in the twilight. It was black with tinted windows. An S-Class model, meaning it would be worth nearly £60,000 new. My eyes were trained on it like a lion's on a gazelle.

Tyler and I were fifty feet away, sitting on a low wall under some trees. I was dying to have a crack at the car. There was no one about. Stodmarsh is a quiet village. Just a few houses and one pub. The Red Lion, down the road from where we sat. It was quiet, but we had to be careful. Two youths, one in a bedraggled suit, the other in a hoodie and trackie bottoms, were going to look out of place.

The Merc sat outside a house, just a stroll from the pub. It was a posh house, covered in ivy, set back from the road. Trees sheltered it. The windows were dark. There was something sinister about the building, and it made me shiver.

Rich owners, I thought.

I envied them. I hated them. I came to steal what they'd worked for, what they'd stolen from the poor. That's how I justified my actions. They were thieves like me. And they had insurance. They'd be all right.

My blood was up. The Merc would be mine. I licked my lips, excited at the prospect.

The same feeling I always got when I was twocking raced through me – I was scared, I was keyed up.

I was Taking Without Owner's Consent.

Expensive new cars like this one were usually quite difficult to steal. There's hi-tech equipment these days that make a twockers work difficult. It was better to go for slightly older vehicles.

With most cars, though, new or old, you had to depend on one thing more than any other.

The owner's stupidity.

And we had it here.

As we waited down the road, sitting on a wall, two big blokes came out of the house and down the path. One of them aimed the key fob at the car and the car bleeped, its lights flashing.

My heart jumped.

Now we wanted the bloke with the key to be a moron.

Tyler was saying, "Come on, mate, come on… "

Even if he left the door open, it would help. We could have a try at hotwiring the car. Like I said, new cars were tough to start.

But you could get past any problem if you knew how.

And we knew how.

The first big bloke got into the driver's seat. He switched on the engine and revved it. Smooth and clean.

"Sounds beautiful," said Tyler.

I agreed.

The second bloke opened the boot.

A chill ran down my spine. The man seemed to baulk, and I sensed his fear. For some reason, I nearly told Tyler to forget it. Something didn't feel right. I did reach for his arm, ready to tell him I wasn't happy.

But I didn't. I should have.

The second bloke counted something in the boot – and he counted to thirteen.

The briefcases. Full of cash. They had to be.

35

Any thoughts of jacking it in dwindled. I was staying put. We were going through with it. The car would be ours, as well as the briefcases and what they contained.

The bloke in the driver's seat turned the engine off before getting out of the car. He said something to the other fella, and they both laughed.

The other man slapped his mate on the shoulder and shut the boot.

Tyler and me were jazzed. We were stiff with nerves. We jangled. Without looking at each other, without saying a word, we were both thinking the same thing:

Don't turn back, mate, don't turn back – walk away from the car, walk away from the car.

They did just that – walked away from the car and towards the house.

Tyler nudged me.

"He did it," he said, "he actually did it."

He did. The fool left the keys in the ignition.

Stupidity. It's a beautiful thing.

It's fate, I thought. This was meant to be. *The car's mine, and the money – and then I can win Sammie back.*

We moved quickly. People can realize they've made a mistake in seconds so you had to be on the ball.

Ten yards from the car, we stopped.

Tyler said, "You up for this?"

My throat was dry but I nodded.

I walked towards the car, and Tyler followed.

At the door, my legs nearly buckled.

"I love stupid people," I said.

I could barely contain my excitement.

I opened the door.

The alarm screamed.

36

I froze, deafened by the noise. How had the alarm gone off if the keys were in the ignition and the car was unlocked?

Then I noticed that attached to the wall next to the Mercedes was a small, plastic box. A red light blinked on the unit. It was an image sensor trained on the vehicle. Any movement around the car triggered it. The high-pitched squeal coming from the device hurt my ears.

Tyler and me were frozen by the din.

Suddenly, through the shrieking alarm, came the sound of men shouting, and the two blokes charged out of the house towards us.

CHAPTER 11.
JUST IN TIME.

I WAS always just in time.

Just in time getting back to my chair after drawing a penis on the blackboard, the teacher storming through the classroom door and screaming, "Who's responsible for that?"

Just in time flinging the magazine back under the bed and pulling up my trousers up before my aunt or Nan came into my bedroom saying, "You okay, Jimmy? You look flustered."

Just in time I bolting through the door, the shop owner hitting the alarm and locking the doors behind me as I raced down the street, beer under my coat.

Just in time – that's how things were for me.

You get away with things often enough, you start to believe you're invincible. You start to believe in God or angels, and that they're looking out for you. You start to believe in luck and in your own ability to get away with stuff.

You start to believe in just in time.

I needed just in time right now.

I needed my hands to stop shaking and Tyler to stop screeching in my ear. I needed to get the car started because those two blokes, as big and burly as silverbacks, were bounding towards us.

I glanced in the rear-view mirror. For a moment, I hesitated. You normally see anger in someone's eyes when you're nicking their car. But that's not what I saw when I looked at the two blokes running towards us right now.

I saw fear.

Absolute dread.

Their eyes were saying, *If this car gets stolen we are in deep, deep trouble*.

"Get it going, Jimmy, get it going!"

Tyler's panicked squeal snapped me out of it, and I started the car just as the thugs were leaping for at the vehicle.

I screeched off down road. Laughter filled the car. Tyler went mental, bouncing up and down in the passenger seat, whooping and hollering.

"We did it, we did it," he was yelping.

But I didn't share his enthusiasm. As I raced through Stodmarsh, heading back towards Canterbury, I took one last look behind me.

The two silverbacks were on their knees.

One of them was on all fours, hammering the ground.

It looked like they were praying.

Why would someone pray when their car got nicked?

It was only a car.

Then two more blokes burst out of the gate and into the street.

My blood ran cold and I nearly lost control of the Mercedes.

These fellas had guns.

The barrels flashed as they fired in our direction, and a split second later gunfire barked and bullets raked the car.

I screamed. Tyler ducked. We swerved all over the road.

The men kept shooting.

CHAPTER 12.
CARS AND GIRLS.

"WE should take it back," I said.

"You what?"

"We should definitely take it back."

"It's got bullet holes in it, now – they won't want it."

"I bet they will."

"No way, Jimmy."

"Then we should dump it."

"We will," said Tyler. "But only after we've had some fun."

"No, we should dump it now."

I kept glancing in my mirrors. I had the feeling we were going to be followed. The people who owned this car weren't the type to phone the cops. They had guns, so they wouldn't want cops around. They were the type who would sort something like this out themselves. And I didn't like mixing with those who sorted things out for themselves. They were usually dangerous.

"They had guns," I said.

Tyler said nothing. He stared ahead. I drove along the Littlebourne Road at a steady 40mph. On my right stood the barracks of the Argyll and Sutherland Highlanders. I thought for a moment about having the army behind me. It would be helpful right now.

I drove sensibly. I didn't want to draw attention to myself, to the car. It was my instinct to keeps the cops at bay, but I started to think it might be a good idea to have them around.

Cops and soldiers backing me up.

I had a feeling I would need them.

"They had guns, Tyler," I repeated.

"Yeah." He was still staring ahead. "That's why I don't think it's a good idea to take the car back. I don't think that'll make any difference. I don't see them saying, 'Thanks for bringing it back, off you go, lads.' I can't see that happening."

"Then we'll dump it."

"We nicked it for a reason, Jimmy. I want to make good use of it. It's a Merc, after all."

My nerves tightened. "You're… you're not doing a job with it or anything?"

"I want to use it to pick up a girl, Jimmy."

"You want to pick up a girl, go on the bus."

"No, I… she's… she's special, right. So I need this car. This special car."

"Go steal another one. One that's not owned by people with guns."

"It's a Merc. I need a flash car for this bird. She's… she's playing hard to get, you know."

I stopped on double yellow lines opposite a Londis store. "You made me nick this car so you could pull a bird?"

He shrugged. "Part of the reason, but… but I didn't want you to… to disappear."

"Disappear, what do you mean?"

"We've been mates for years, and… and I like us being mates."

I said nothing. I wasn't sure if I did like it anymore.

He went on. "And if you were going to, you know, stop doing stuff with me, we'd stop being mates."

"We can't be mates based on stealing cars and racing them round town, Tyler. I want to be a driver. I want to race for real. I really think I should stop while I'm ahead – while I haven't got a stint at a young offenders' institution, or worse, prison, behind me. No one will want to hire me or trust me if I've been inside. And… and Sammie, she's not going to take me back."

"So… she has dumped you, then?" his eyes brightened.

"I'm glad you're pleased about it."

He blushed. "I'm not. Just… just surprised. You were, like, for life."

"She's given me the cold shoulder today. She said it's over. But… you know. It hurts in here, Tyler." I rubbed my chest where missing her ached. "I want her back. She's… she's good for me, and I love her."

He looked away. Love was grubby for the lads. They didn't get why I only wanted to be with Sammie. But she made my heart leap. She made my skin tingle. I was excited every time I saw her and when I wasn't with her, it felt like there was a big hole in my chest.

Tyler said, "You're lucky to have a bird like Sammie."

"You think so?"

He looked me straight in the eye. His expression was serious. Tyler was never serious. He was usually mad or funny. "'Course I think so. She's… she's great."

"Yeah, she is great. That's why I want her back."

"Okay, I get it. But… but I'd give it a few hours."

I narrowed my eyes. "Since when did you give advice on girlfriends?"

He went red. "I… I'm just saying."

I didn't want to knock him down. He was lonely. Tyler never really had a proper girlfriend. Girls never liked him much. He was plain-looking. He carried a little too much weight and his skin was bad. He looked a bit like Matt Lucas, but with hair.

I'm not sure if he wanted a proper girlfriend, like I had Sammie, or just someone he could mention down the pub: "Yeah, my bird does this… " or, "My bird went to so and so… "

Having a good-looking girl on your arm gives your ego a boost, it increases your swagger. I was like that with Sammie when I started going out with her. She was a real fox, like my dad said quietly sometimes when he saw a nice woman on TV. Or he'd say, "Your mum was a real fox before the cancer got to her," and then he'd start to shake, trying to bite back the tears.

I liked strutting about with Sammie.

Everyone knew I was going out with her. Everyone was jealous.

But then, very quickly, I started to fall for her. Really get to love her. My blood fizzing when I saw her. My skin tingling and sweating.

I wanted to be with her all the time – all the time. And that pissed my mates off.

They called me ghost. I was always missing. And Tyler moaned about it the most.

Finally, I decided I had to strike a balance – girlfriend and mates. I tried my best. But it wasn't enough for the lads, for Tyler especially.

I was a fool. I sided with my mates too much. I tried to do the right thing, but it's difficult when you're seventeen and you don't really know what's going on.

Looking back, I made the wrong choice – spent too much time with Tyler, particularly, which led me to lose Sammie.

But right then I felt hopeful. I was going to win Sammie back. I was going to stop stealing cars and learn to drive them properly instead. Learn to race them around circuits and get paid for it.

I looked at Tyler and felt sorry for him – no girlfriend, no prospects. A vision went through my head:

Ten years from now, me living in Monte Carlo with Sammie. I'm coming back to England for the British Grand Prix at Brands

Hatch. I win the race and I'm F1 world champion. I wave to the crowd. And there in the sea of faces is a chubby, acned, bald bloke, just a fan, just a nobody – just Tyler.

"You can take the Merc," I said to him. "But be careful. Don't get nicked. Take your bird out. But after you're done, dump this thing. Get rid of it. The cops will be looking for it soon. Or worse, the blokes we nicked it from. Just be careful."

"What… what about the briefcases?"

The briefcases. I thought about it for a few second.

Then I said, "Leave them. Don't touch them. We don't need to know anything about them. Just dump it after you're done. Burn it if you can."

I got out of the car.

"I'll give you a ride back," he said.

"No, I'll walk or catch a bus. I need to clear my head."

As he drove away, Tyler made the tires screech on the road. I squirmed. The Mercedes sped off.

Bullet holes peppered the boot and the back bumper. I grew hot with fear, recalling the dangerous people we were dealing with.

But I didn't know then just how dangerous.

CHAPTER 13.
YOU HAVE TO RUN.

WHEN I got home, the house was empty. I stood in the living room door, squinting. Not like Dad. He was usually parked in his chair at this time of the evening, coming up to 8.00pm, all the soaps on TV.

I don't know why he liked the soaps so much. I suppose it was because their lives were exciting. His wasn't. His life was dull and broken.

Sometimes I worried about Dad killing himself. It scared me, and I tried not to think about it. But it was a possibility. What would I do if I lost Sammie, if she died of cancer and I'd never get her back?

Panic set in when I thought of my dad dying. I'd feel lost. Although we never spent any time together, and I wasn't sure if I wanted to, Dad not being there would be weird. He was a lifejacket. He stopped me from sinking down all the way to the bottom. He held me up, and I never thanked him for it.

I went to the kitchen. The smell of lasagne lingered in the air. I flicked the light switch, but nothing happened. I kept flicking it. Still nothing happened.

I tutted. In the gloom, I went to the fridge and opened it. Milk, cheese, and an open packet of ham. I ate the ham in the dark, thinking about my dad, thinking about Sammie, and thinking about Tyler and hoping he'd be able to pull this girl.

The Merc came to mind.

A cold sweat broke on my back.

Dump the Mercedes after you've done, mate, I thought. *Just get rid of it.*

What kind of people owned that car?

Panic squeezed my heart. My appetite disappeared, and I felt dizzy and sick with the ham in my belly, wanting to throw it up.

I remembered the guns.

Christ, how could I have forgotten the guns.

I was so complacent. So stupid.

Dad's absence started to worry me.

My legs felt weak. My belly wrenched.

What if the men with guns had identified Tyler and me and had kidnapped my dad and Tyler's mum?

They would torture them. They would kill them.

I wanted a piss and panted for air. I was hot and sweaty. I rushed upstairs. Halfway up my phone rang. It was Dad.

"Dad, you okay?" I said.

There was two seconds of silence before he said, "What have you done, mate? What have you done this time?"

"Dad, where... where are you?"

"I'm up the allotment."

"You okay?"

He said nothing.

"Dad, you okay?"

"The police came round earlier."

I almost said, *Yeah I saw them and legged it,* but I stayed quiet.

Dad said, "I told them I had no clue where my son was. It was the truth. I didn't have a clue. They weren't impressed, son."

"No, sorry."

46

"Sorry," he said and blew air out of his cheeks. "No more sorry, Jimmy. Sorry doesn't help now. What have you done?"

"Missed curfew, Dad. Big deal." I was relieved. I thought he might have been kidnapped by those gunmen. I thought he was being brutalized. But it was only the cops irritated by me missing curfew – so what? I'd be back in front of the beak tomorrow – the rat-face, probably. He'd give me a warning. Or perhaps he'd send me to a young offenders' unit. Yesterday that would've scared me. Now I didn't care. It was better than Dad being dead.

And anyway, if Sammie had dumped me, there was no point in life.

I had hoped to win her back. But if I was going down, I'd stand no chance. It was pointless worrying about it.

Dad hadn't been kidnapped. He wasn't being tortured. No one was going to shoot him.

I'd stroll into the police station tomorrow and say, "It's a fair cop," let them cuff me and take me to court.

My mind prepared for incarceration.

And jail wasn't so bad.

I knew blokes who'd been inside – Standford Hill on Sheppey, mostly. It's a D-Cat prison. An open prison. Minor offences. I know a few guys who've been sent to B-Cat and C-Cat nicks. That's more serious.

I'd be sent to Cookham Wood, the juvenile prison near Rochester. A couple of my mates had been there. They'd swanned about, playing pool and going to the gym, and came out fitter and up for more trouble.

One of those blokes went back inside for murder a couple of years later. He's not coming out anytime soon. He glassed a lad in a pub fight, slicing open his jugular. Stamped on the fella's head while the poor sod was bleeding to death. I don't remember him being a nutter before he went to Rochester. Prison hardened him. It might harden me, too.

47

But I didn't care. I had no choice but not to care. And that's what I told my dad: "They can sod off. What's the worst that can happen?"

My dad stayed quiet for a second, and it made me worry.

And then he said some words that terrified me:

"You have to run," he said.

"What?"

"You have to run. Get as far away as possible."

His voice was shaking. I'd never heard him like this before. My dad was scared.

My skin goose fleshed.

"Dad, what are you talking about?"

"Come here quickly. I've got some money here for you. Something to tide you over. Help you get away."

"Dad, get away from who?"

He whimpered. "You shouldn't have nicked that Mercedes, son."

"How... how do you know about the Merc?"

He said nothing.

Guns and torture and gangsters plagued my mind.

CHAPTER 14.
PAYMENT.

HE was sitting in the shed with a bottle of gin, half drunk.

"Dad," I said, "I'm scared. What's going on?"

The shed smelled of soil. Dad sat on a barrel. I stood near the door. The cold came inside and chilled me.

He drank from the bottle. I could've done with a swig, but I stayed quiet, waiting for him to answer.

"You've done a stupid thing this time, Jimmy," he said.

"Is it those cops? I saw them at the house earlier and legged it."

"The cops would be nothing, son. This isn't the cops."

"Dad." I slumped to the floor, feeling all my strength leaving me. "Dad, they… the people who owned the Mercedes… they had guns, Dad."

He groaned. He looked pale. He looked older than he'd looked before.

"Are they coming after us?" I said, fear chilling my blood.

He took another drink.

"Are they coming after us with guns?" I said.

"Son, guns are the least of your trouble."

I tried to say something, but no words came out.

Dad looked at his watch.

"It's nearly nine o'clock," he said.

"W-what happens at nine o'clock?"

49

He shook his head. "We never took you to church when you were a boy, did we?"

"What are you talking about?" I stood up. I was getting panicky. "Dad, you're – "

He lifted a hand and stopped me. "We should have. Your mum wanted to, bless her. But I'd say, 'It's a waste of time. Let him play football with his mates'. She would tut and go back to making the dinner."

I tried to speak again, but before I could say anything, Dad was jabbering:

"Your mum, she believed in… in Jesus and God and all that. She's in heaven now; I don't doubt that. She was good, your mum. Kind to everyone. But… but you know, if there is a God and heaven there's also… there's also something else, Jimmy."

I thought I knew what he was saying but didn't want to listen, didn't want to hear.

But he went on:

"Everything has a reflection, doesn't it. Mum was my reflection. I suppose Sammie, she was your reflection. And heaven… heaven is hell's reflection – "

"Dad, did the car belong to gangsters or drug dealers or – "

"Worse," he said, spitting. "Much, much worse. After the police came, I was thinking: *that's it, I've got to sort my son out – no more nicking cars. He'll get into trouble, big time*. But just as I was thinking that, cooking my lasagne, there you were getting into trouble – big time."

I was shaking. Was my dad going mad? Was he just drunk?

"How… how do you know about the Mercedes, Dad?"

"Because he came to tell me about it."

"Who?" My mind reeled. Was it Tyler who told him? Had he driven over to my dad's house with the Merc after he'd left me?

"The one whose car you stole," said my dad.

I was hot, but my skin was cold. I was a bag of nerves. I could feel myself falling into this deep, deep chasm, from where I could never escape.

"Whose car did we steal, Dad?"

"It's not the car, son. You've stolen something much, much more valuable than the car." Tears rolled down his cheeks. "I love you, son."

I gawped.

He said, "I should have told you that years ago, and not let you get away with things. I should have been tougher."

"Dad… "

"You have to go," he said. From his pocket he took a thick, brown envelope. "There's money there. A grand. It'll get you away from here. Get you somewhere."

I stared at the envelope.

"Take it," Dad said.

It wasn't like me to turn down cash, but I just couldn't take it.

Dad jabbed the envelope towards me. "You have to take it and go. I've paid for you. Made payment. But if he finds you, it won't matter."

"You've paid? Paid what? Paid who? You got more cash than this?"

"I haven't paid with money, Jimmy."

Just then, the sound of wind battering sails filled the air, and shadows flashed past the window making the darkness darker.

"What's that?" I said.

I glanced out of the window and saw something that made my insides turn into water.

Dad rose, fear on his face. He threw the cash at me.

"Son," he said, "you stay in this shed and keep out of sight – and whatever happens, do not come out until he's gone. He will destroy you."

CHAPTER 15.
FIGHTING FOR SAM.

I'M not a tough guy, but I'd fight for Sam. Running was usually my answer to trouble. It was a successful form of self-defence. I was lean and nimble, so I could out-sprint most bullies – and that included coppers and teachers, too.

I've only been physically involved in one fight. The others I've run away from. That's probably why I'm still alive. Kids I know use knives. Kids who threatened me and started on me before I legged it.

Let them call me a coward. Who cares? I was alive and un-injured – and that's how Sammie liked me to be.

But I did fight for her once.

It was about a year ago. We were still at school. I was nearly leaving. Mind you, I'd been leaving since I was about thirteen.

Sammie was being bullied by a girl called Jackie-Ann Furlong.

Jackie-Ann Furlong was a thug. She was a big girl. Tall and wide. She shoved everyone around – girls and boys.

Sammie always got picked on because she was pretty and popular. She was feisty as well and managed to fend off most bullying campaigns launched against her.

That was until Jackie-Ann came along.

She and her mum and brother had moved from London and lived down the road from me.

Her old man was in jail for armed robbery. Two of her brothers were inside for assault.

Her younger brother, Jordan, was in Year 10, same as Sammie. He was built like a battleship, and no one messed with him.

Schools don't really deal with bullying until someone kicks up a fuss in the papers or on TV. They don't want to know because it can damage their reputation and affect their standing in league tables.

So no one ever gets bullied at school despite the fact that they do, every day, every week, all the time.

For some reason, Jackie-Ann Furlong took a shine to me. It was pretty bad luck. Her last boyfriend had been a few years older than her and went inside with her dad for that armed robbery.

She was obviously heartbroken, and I would be her rebound.

She made it quite clear Sammie needed to get out of the way, or she'd cut her face.

Her words were, "If you don't get out of my way, I'll cut your Barbie Doll face to ribbons, your bitch."

Sammie doesn't take any crap, and she stood up to Jackie-Ann. You usually front up to bullies, and they back down.

But not Jackie-Ann Furlong.

She shoved Sammie into a wall, and the impact gave her concussion and a nasty cut.

I was raging, but Sammie told me, "Just leave it for now."

"I can't leave it," I said, shaking with rage.

"Do it for me. I'm fine."

She was fine until Jackie-Ann started picking on her again.

Jackie-Ann warned her off, saying I was now going out with her, and if she ever saw Sammie with me again, she'd burn her house down.

Sammie told her teachers. Jackie-Ann was hauled in and denied everything. The teachers swept it under the carpet. Jackie-Ann got mad. Nothing a family of crooks hate more than a grass. And Sammie was a grass.

The bullying got worse. I spoke to my dad about it. I was hoping he'd say, "Stand up for her, mate." But instead he told me, "Don't get involved – especially not over a girl."

I finally confronted Jackie-Ann and said, "I'd never going out with you, not even if you were the last girl on earth. And if you lay a hand on Sammie again, I'll break into your house and have it cleared out."

She went pale. I doubt if Jackie-Ann Furlong had ever been threatened.

She had now, and she didn't like it.

From white, her face went to red.

She fumed and swore at me, saying that me and my "slag girlfriend" would be smashed to pieces before the end of the day.

Jackie-Ann's threats were heard by a teacher, who gave her detention. So that got her out of the way. But as she was being dragged off to the headmaster's office, she turned and shouted, "I'll get Jordan on you and that bitch. Tonight, the both of you. Dead… "

That's when I fought my first fight.

And it wasn't against any old lout. It was against Jordan Furlong, six-two, sixteen stone, undefeated in playground and parks.

Sammie was under threat, so I had to stand up for her. I had no choice.

I'd like to say I won the fight, but I didn't. Jordan Furlong beat me up. I got a few punches in, but nothing to bother him.

I might not have won the fight, but I did win the day.

And I saved Sammie.

I was on a curfew at the time – again. I met Jordan Furlong after school in the local park at 6.00pm. I wasn't supposed to be there. If I got nicked, I'd be back in court.

Jordan Furlong was also on probation at the time. He'd beaten up a kid a few weeks before. Not the first time he'd assaulted someone, but he'd been warned it would be the last time. Next time he'd be in juvenile prison.

But for Jordan and me, and most kids like us, there was never a last time.

You never thought about the consequences.

You never thought you'd get caught.

But Jordan was about to.

Moments before I went to face him, I made a call to the cops.

I pretended to be someone else and reported myself for being out after curfew.

We squared up, a crowd of kids watching us.

Sammie was there, crying. I'd told her not to worry: "I've got it sorted."

But she still cried and tried to stop me going ahead.

Jordan said, "After I smash you, I'll smash your tart."

That made me angry. I bunched my fists. That just made him laugh. He came at me like a bull.

Just as Jordan Furlong was getting close to killing me, sirens blared.

Cops swarmed the park.

He was arrested, kicking off as usual, throwing punches at the coppers.

I was taken to hospital. A few days later, my eyes black and my ribs aching, I was up in front of the magistrates' for breaking my curfew.

The beak sympathized with me and gave me another chance.

Furlong was sent to juvenile prison. His family were evicted from their council house. They went back to London, as far as I knew.

But I'd fought for Sammie. And she was grateful.

She cried over me in hospital and said I was her hero.

I would fight anyone for her. I'd do it again and again.

And I was about to learn that I would have to.

But this adversary would make Jordan Furlong look like Snoopy.

This adversary wasn't even human.

And it was about to kill my dad.

CHAPTER 16.
AFTER THE EXECUTION.

FOR a second, I gawped as my dad's body slumped to the ground.

His head rolled away into the furrows in the soil.

My eyes filled with tears.

Then the dark, winged man hurtled towards the shed. His eyes were red. He was naked, and his skin was pale.

I ducked down, expecting him to smash through the window. I'd be dead. But in that moment I didn't care. My dad was gone. Sammie had dumped me. I was going to prison.

What was the point in living.

My dad had gone outside and told me to stay put when the winged man had landed in the allotment.

At first I didn't know what the flapping sound was – it sounded like wind on sail.

But when I glanced out of the window, I saw the winged man land, his black wings easing him to earth.

They were huge wings. Of course, I had nothing to compare them to – I'd never seen a man with wings before.

But they were twice as tall as him, and leathery, like the wings of pterodactyls you see in dinosaur movies.

I knew straight away who he was. It dawned on me because of what dad had been saying about heaven and stuff.

This winged man was an angel.

An angel of death.

As he sailed towards me, I prayed. I'd never prayed before.

But after my dad had rambled on about God, I thought it might be worth it.

I begged Jesus, God, and St Peter to save me.

And just when I expected the angel to burst through the window, I heard a whooshing sound. A shadow passed across the window, blocking out the night sky.

The winged man rocketed upwards.

His wings lashed the night. He climbed up and up, and he got smaller and smaller until he was gone.

I waited in the shed for a while, whimpering, feeling more scared than I'd ever felt in my life.

Finally I struggled to my feet and went out to my father's dead body.

I knelt there and cried.

"Dad, Dad, please… "

But it was pointless. It wasn't like he'd suffered a heart attack, and you could pray for him to open his eyes. It wasn't like any disease got him, and he could maybe be cured.

My dad had no head.

His eyes were still open and looking at me, and his mouth was agape – as if he'd been stunned by his own death.

I didn't know what to do.

Phone 999 – and tell them what?

"My dad's just got his head cut off by a man with wings."

Like that would work.

I'd be arrested and blamed for it.

But maybe I was to blame.

Maybe I'd killed my dad.

My stupid, childish, ignorant behaviour had resulted in his death.

Then I remembered his words:

I've paid for you.

What did that mean?

I kept crying, confused and hurt and grieving.

Paid for what?

The money, I thought suddenly. The money my dad was going to give me. I started to head back for the shed where I'd left it, but then my phone rang.

Tyler's ID came up on the screen.

I answered and was about to cry out that my dad was dead when his voice, also full of panic and tears, said, "I'm so sorry, Jimmy, I'm so sorry, but they've taken Sammie, and it's my fault. They've taken her."

CHAPTER 17.
WHAT'S IN THE BOOT?

"SO the girl you wanted to pull was Sam," I said.

I was mad. I wanted to hit Tyler. My fists were bunched, ready to lay into him.

"I'm really sorry, mate," he said, tears running down his face. "It was just... I... I don't know – "

"Forget it. We've got to find her. Who took her?"

"Big guys. Guys like the ones we saw outside the house."

My blood ran cold.

Tyler whined on: "We were parked up, right. Just off the Whitstable Road. I... I was hoping for a... for a snog – "

"I don't want to know."

"I'm only saying what happened."

"Just what happened. Not what you *hoped* was going to happen."

"Okay, okay... well... we were parked up, like I said... "

He blustered and flapped. I was thinking, *Get on with it before I lamp you.*

We were parked on Giles Lane, off the University of Kent campus. It was just near where Tyler had tried to get off with Sammie. It was about ten-fifteen. We were pacing round the car. It was cold, but I was hot with rage and grief. Tyler was a bag of nerves, whining like a baby.

He had rung me, crying, saying Sammie had been taken and then said he was too scared to go anywhere, please could I come to him.

He begged and begged, and he was hysterical. He couldn't drive, he said. He was too scared.

So I got the bus to Giles Lane.

I was so wound up by the time I got there.

The road was dark and quiet. Now and again students traipsed back to their digs. The odd car would drive by.

I hadn't told Tyler about my father's murder. The event still burned in me. It made tears come to my eyes. It made my heart feel as if it was going to burst. It felt like a nightmare, and maybe it was – maybe when I got home my dad would be there watching Corrie.

"So then," Tyler continued, "Sam, she leaps out of the car after I… "

He tailed off.

I finished his sentence for him. "After you tried to get off with her."

"Yeah, okay… "

"Then what?"

"Then I get out to go after her, say sorry – "

I was ready to hit him, but I hit the Merc instead and hurt my fist. The pain made pins and needles go through me. I snarled, hugging my hand under my armpit.

"Then," said Tyler, retreating, "this van appears. Black. Headlights blinding me. Two blokes jump out. Suits. Big guys. Like the ones we saw, but not them. Sam screams and freezes. I tell her to run, and I get back in the car. The men rush up to her. By then, I'm in the car – "

"Coward," I growled, wanting to throw another punch – this time at Tyler's face.

"No… no, mate… it was too late… they grabbed her and then… then I… they were coming for me, for the car and I… "

"You left her. You drove away, came here and hid. Too scared to move. Too much of a coward to go looking for her."

"I'm… I'm sorry. That's… that's why I don't deserve someone like… like Sam."

"You don't deserve anyone at all – you're completely useless. You're just no good, Tyler, and you've never been any good."

He recoiled as if I'd smacked him. I *should've* smacked him, to be honest. I wanted to, badly. The itch to deck him was terrible. And he knew it.

"You want to hit me, don't you," he said.

"Yes."

"Do it then, because I deserve it."

"Someone killed Dad."

Tyler gawped.

I told him what I'd seen.

He was still gawping when I finished telling him, and after a few seconds he said, "Angel of death?"

We were quiet for a while.

Then I remembered something and said, "Did you ever check those briefcases?"

"What?"

"My dad told me we'd stolen something much more valuable than this Merc."

We both looked at the boot of the car.

"Let's see," I said.

A minute later we were standing over the unopened boot, staring at it like we didn't know what to do. It was pitted with bullet holes. An odd smell came from the cavities. A sweet odour that made me a bit hazy

"So… so are we going to open it?" said Tyler.

He looked sheepish. He was embarrassed about what happened with Sam. I had thought he fancied her. Who wouldn't? And in fact it made me proud that my mates eyed my girlfriend.

But I only wanted them to look – not try to touch.

He'd betrayed me. He'd lied to me about using the Merc to pull a bird when all along the bird was Sammie.

I asked him, "Did you plan to nick this Merc so you could pull Sam? Had that been your plan?"

His eyes went wide. "No, mate. Only… when you broke up I thought, well… I thought… "

"Even if we had broken up – "

"You have – "

"We've had a row – "

"You've – "

"Even if we had, Tyler, you should've asked. Or said. It's… it's the right thing to do."

He shrugged and mumbled something that sounded like sorry.

I tutted and opened the boot.

We froze.

I counted them – thirteen black leather briefcases piled neatly in the boot. They had gold clasps and gold ID tags. On each tag was some lettering in a language I'd never seen before. I licked my lips.

"Sh…shall we open one?" said Tyler. "M…maybe there's cash inside."

Cash, I thought. I'd left the money my dad was going to give me in the shed. I could do with some dough, do what my dad told me to do and escape.

Maybe the Merc's owners were gangsters after all. Maybe the angel of death had just been a figment of my imagination.

They were just normal bank robbers or drug dealers.

I almost felt relieved.

"What do you think?" said Tyler.

"I think we're in the shit."

And then something terrible came to my mind.

Sammie.

They had Sammie.

And my skin crawled at the thought of her imprisoned by those thugs.

"We've got to find Sam," I said.

Tyler did his gawping thing again.

"Give me the keys," I said. "I'm driving."

As I took the bunch from Tyler, my phone rang.

My heart lurched. Two names came to mind – my dad and Sam.

I took out my phone. The name on the ID screen filled me with hope. It was her name – her lovely, beautiful name.

I answered the phone, "Sam, are you okay?"

"Mr Jimmy Chance?" said a voice so cold and slimy it made me shiver as it slithered into my ears, deep into my brain.

CHAPTER 18.
THREATS.

MY mouth was dry and I failed to speak.

Tyler was saying, "Who is it?" but the look of horror on my face suggested that whoever it was, he might be better off backing away – and that's what he did.

I stared at him. He was such a coward. I never thought Tyler would stand by me. He wasn't going to surprise me.

The voice on the phone said, "You have something of mine. Something that belongs to my master. I want it back, Mr Chance. I want it back, or what happened to your father happens to this delicious little cake I have here."

I heard Sam scream.

I wanted to leap down the phone.

"Don't hurt her, or I'll kill you," I said, never having uttered anything like that to anyone, not even knowing how I'd do such a thing.

The voice laughed. "You are such a small, meaningless thing, Jimmy," he said.

"You killed my dad."

"Yes, I did."

"You… you promised not to. He… he told me… " I was crying. "He… he paid a price."

"The price was his death. His soul."

I said nothing for a few seconds, just digesting what he'd told me:

Soul?

Then I said, "So… so you've got that, let Sam go, and you can have what you want. You can have the car back. Let us go."

There was a pause. I looked at Tyler. He was ten yards away from me, as if the phone call would infect him if he came any closer.

Then the voice said, "You just don't know what you are dealing with, Jimmy. You are beyond redemption now. Beyond making deals."

"I won't tell the cops. I don't like the cops. I'm not a grass."

He laughed again. "I don't care about your authorities. I don't care for earthly things at all. But you, Jimmy, have transgressed terribly. You have taken something that you should not have taken."

"Well, I've always taken things I shouldn't have taken."

"You should've learned your lesson, then."

"J-J-Jimmy… " It was Tyler. He was whimpering. I couldn't be bothered looking at him. I never wanted to look at him again. "J-J-Jimmy… "

"I am sending someone to collect what you took from me."

"And bringing Sam back."

"No – "

"Well, you're not having what you want then."

"I think I am."

"JIMMY!"

Tyler's scream made me look up. I was about to tell him to shut up when I saw what he'd seen.

Hurtling down road came something that looked like a fireball.

I blinked, hoping it would get rid of the nightmare vision.

But it was still there when my eyes were open again. And it was closer.

The voice on the phone laughed like a lunatic. I cut him off, stuffing the phone back into my pocket.

Tyler screamed and raced for the car, and I followed him.

I looked back just as the huge chariot with wheels of fire, spraying sparks everywhere, roared past a row of cars.

They were immediately charred.

Two monstrous black horses with blood-red eyes pulled the chariot. Steam plumed from their nostrils. Spit flew from their mouths. Their hooves tore up the road.

The earth shook and Tyler and me found it difficult to stay on our feet, but we got into the car and shut the doors and I started the engine.

The rider in the chariot was a hooded thing brandishing a whip.

He cracked it and it lashed out and came alongside the car. Blood and flesh clung to it, and then it was gone.

Tyler screamed for me to get going. I put the Merc into gear and shot away, tires screeching.

I glanced in the rear-view mirror.

The chariot and the horses straight from hell followed us.

CHAPTER 19.
HELL ON OUR HEELS.

AT the junction leading out in the Whitstable Road, I never stopped. I shot out without looking. Car horns blared. Tires screeched. Headlights flashed. I swung left towards Canterbury.

Tyler screamed in my ear. His panic was infectious. Terror gripped me. Had I seen what I thought I'd seen?

It had to be real.

Tyler had seen it as well.

But I still found it difficult to believe.

Perhaps it was a trick. Someone driving along in a van or a truck nearby transmitting the image of the fiery chariot and the monstrous horses onto the sky.

That had to be it.

I glanced in the rear-view mirror.

The chariot was behind us.

"It's coming," shouted Tyler, jumping up and down in the seat next to me, "it's still coming, Jimmy."

And it was. Ploughing along the A290. Churning up the asphalt. Tossing other vehicles aside.

"Ring 999," I told Tyler.

He screamed.

"Ring the 999, Tyler."

"You what?"

"Ring 999."

Tyler never expected those words to come out of my mouth, but I was desperate.

My hands were sweaty on the steering wheel. My driving was crazy.

I raced downhill into a built-up area. Cars lined the street. Traffic was quite heavy. It was a Friday night, cabs on fares and people going home from a night out.

Behind me the chariot scythed through everything in its path.

Tyler was shouting in my ear. His screams put my teeth on edge. I was panicking. But if we were going to survive, I had to concentrate.

My eyes stayed on the road most of the time, but now and again I glanced in my mirrors and there was blazing chariot pursuing me.

Hell was on our heels.

And it was gaining on us.

I floored the accelerator. The needle climbed. The engine purred. It was a beautiful car.

Tyler screamed. He bobbed up and down in his seat. He was squealing that he was going to shit himself and for me to get him out of there, but I could only just understand him.

We were reaching 90mph. Crazy speeds in a residential area. I slammed the horn, warning traffic and pedestrians to get out of our way.

Ahead of me, it was havoc. Cars were swerving out of the road as I approached. People stood and stared at what was following me.

I weaved round obstacles – cars, bikes, trucks.

The chariot went through them.

I thought, *People are dying – and I'm going to get blamed.*

Terror filled my heart. I started to think that no way the cops would believe what was happening. I would be blamed.

But perhaps it wasn't happening. Perhaps I was hallucinating. My father's death had made me snap and temporarily lose my mind.

I wished that were true.

I wished the chariot would disappear and the horses fade into the night.

But they stayed their course. They kept coming. The wheels spinning and spraying fire. The charioteer's whip lashing out. The horses' hooves tearing up the road. Their breath yellow in the gloom, their eyes burning red.

My heart thundered.

"We're going to die," shrieked Tyler, "oh, God, we're going to die… " I wished he would shut up. I was shaking, and my hands hurt because my grip on the steering wheel was so tight. My stomach felt queasy, and my head throbbed.

The road narrowed. We were coming towards the city.

The pavements were packed with Friday-nighters. They stopped. They stared. They screamed.

I had slowed, but was still going at 60mph through a 30mph area, forcing cars aside.

The chariot gained on me, driving straight – going through and over everything, leaving a trail of destruction.

Ahead of me lay the city walls. I planned to drive into the town itself and lose the charioteer in the narrow streets.

The lights on the level crossing turned red. A train was leaving Canterbury West for London.

The barrier started to drop.

There was no traffic in front of me. Cars had edged to the side. Some drivers scowled at me. Drunks threw things at the car – cans, bottles and takeaways hit the windscreen.

But then their hate for me turned to fear when they saw what was chasing me. They dived behind their vehicles. The pissheads tried to run away, but stumbled over their drunken feet.

It was hopeless for them all.

As the chariot sped past, cars and people burned in its wake.

Tyler moaned.

I shut my eyes for a second, trying to wipe away the image of charred humans.

The barrier was dropping.

Tyler said, "Train's coming, Jimmy, train!"

I kept driving.

Tyler screamed. The red lights flashed. The barrier was down. I sped up. Tyler screamed. I screamed. I ducked. The train appeared on my left side. I smashed through the barrier. The train loomed. It howled a warning. I yelled out and smashed through the barrier on the other side. The train swept past the back of the car, inches away. I swear I felt it clip the bumper, but really it could have been anything.

The important thing was I got through.

Tyler howled with laughter.

I hooted and shouted with joy. I slowed the car and looked behind me as the train swept by. I just wanted to see that I'd beaten the chariot, that I'd won the race.

I smiled, relieved.

Then the train was cut in half. The horses sliced through. Metal squealed. The carriages lurched. Bits of them flew through the air. Doors. Seating. Passengers. Fire filled the sky. From the flames came the horses and the chariot.

"Drive," screamed Tyler, "drive…"

I cried out and floored the accelerator, heading for the Westgate Towers, the gateway into Canterbury.

I drove straight over the roundabout and shot through the archway, between the drum-shaped towers of the gateway, and into the city.

And hell came too.

CHAPTER 20.
THE FIRST TIME.

I STOLE my first car when I was thirteen. By then I was racing go-karts – and winning races. I raced at Buckmore Park in Chatham. It was where F1 world champions Jenson Button and Lewis Hamilton learned their trade.

The first time I went there, I was nine years old. My uncle took me. He was into racing. He was my dad's brother, but unlike my dad he had jokes. Maybe he had jokes because his wife was still alive.

The family just thought I needed a hobby to keep my mind off my mum's death, so they asked him to take me. I think Nan actually told him he had to take me. Being an F1 fan, I don't think he minded.

Anyway, it was a good hobby. And if you believe in fate, and that one thing leads to another in a long chain of events, then it got me here, with hell on my heels.

I loved karting – the speed, the freedom, and the winning.

Racing competitively, I started coming first – rookie events, junior events. I learned to hate losing. It made me feel sick.

When I was thirteen, my uncle left my auntie and went to live in London. He said, "Sorry, Jimmy, I can't take you to Buckmore anymore."

I asked my dad, but he said, "No, I can't take you. We don't have the money."

I asked my Nan, who said, "Well, I think it's time you forgot about being a little boy, now, Jimmy, and started being a man."

It was a Wednesday. All day at school, I'd moped and sulked. I told Tyler about it, and he said, "You should nick a car. Brandon does it all the time. It's easy. I'll show you how to hotwire one."

It turned out not to be that easy. Not too difficult, but not a doddle.

The worst thing about it was the fear.

You shake. You sweat. You dread.

Especially the first time.

That night, Tyler came round my house about 7.00pm. Nan, who was on her way home after washing up my dinner plate, said, "Make sure you're back by 8.30pm, Jimmy – school tomorrow," and then I heard her tell Dad, "Tell him to be back by 8.30pm."

Dad said nothing, just stared at the telly with a tray of fish fingers and chips on his lap.

I said I'd be back and then, trembling, left with Tyler to look for a car.

"Brandon says it's better to steal older cars," Tyler said. At school that day he'd talked me through the process of hotwiring a car.

Now he went on:

"New cars have all this computer software stuff in them. Get a nice older car, he says. Nicer the better. Quicker the better."

I looked at Tyler. "You're shaking. Are you scared?"

"Me? No way."

"Your eyes are big, and your face is really white, Tyler – you look scared to me."

"I'm not scared, Jimmy. I… I do this all the time with Brandon."

"But Brandon always gets caught. You've never got caught, have you?"

74

"N… no, 'cause I leg it."

"Leaving your brother to face the Old Bill?"

He went red. "N… no… he… just shut up, right, and let's look for a car." He stomped off down the road. I followed.

Looking back, that little chat should have set off alarm bells in my head. If Tyler Jackson was willing to abandon his own flesh and blood to the authorities, he'd not think twice about leaving me behind. And he didn't think twice. Ever.

We scoped a few cars on the estates off the Sturry Road. They were family cars. Fords and Nissans and Vauxhalls. Nothing too flash. Nothing too fast. Nothing too sporty. Two teenagers driving a Lotus might draw attention. You didn't want attention. Not at the start. It was something I got a taste for later on. I wanted the cops to see me. I wanted them to chase me. I wanted to race them and beat them, and mostly I did.

But the first car had to be bland, or at least normal.

We spotted a Honda Jazz. 1.4 engine. Grey. A few years old.

I swallowed, nerves making my throat dry.

"That'll do," I said.

It was a neat little car. Nippy and reasonably cool. Had a few bumps and needed a good scrub. But it was okay. Okay for my first time.

"Give it a shake," said Tyler.

"Why?"

"See if it's got anti-theft devices. If it has, it'll go off – and we leg it."

I nodded. I shoved the car. Tense, I was ready to run. The car stayed silent.

"Hurry, then," said Tyler, licking his lips, eyes skimming around. It was a quiet little close just off Military Road. Council houses. Street lights broken. Trees giving us cover.

I got my ruler out and poked it between the rubber weather-stripping and the door on the driver's side, just above the lock. I swiped it down. Nothing happened. The hairs on the back of my neck tingled.

"Again, again," said Tyler.

I swiped again. Nothing.

"It's not working."

"Keep doing it."

My legs were like jelly. My stomach churned. I was scared. Did I really want to be doing this?

I swiped again.

The lock clicked.

I stepped back and gasped.

"Get in," said Tyler.

We got into the car. I couldn't breathe. I sat behind the wheel, staring at the console and the clocks and everything as if I'd never seen the inside of a vehicle before.

"Come on, come on," Tyler said. "Do it. Like I showed you. Come on, Jimmy."

With a screwdriver, I wrenched off the outer ring of the ignition housing.

Wires spooled out. I found the two red flexes – one supplies power to the ignition switch, the other connects to the car's electrical circuits. I stripped the insulation off the wires and wound them together.

Tyler again was saying, "Come on, come – "

"I'm there," I interrupted. "Just shut it."

I sweated and shook, fear and excitement buzzing through me.

My sweaty fingers found the ignition wire, the brown one, and I stripped about half-and-inch of flex from it.

I licked my dry lips.

I touched the ignition wire to the coiled red ones and –

VROOOOOM...

Tyler and me whooped. I revved the engine so I wouldn't stall. Adrenaline coursed through me. I rammed the car into gear and

76

wheel-spinned out of the parking space, clipping a Vauxhall Safira as I went. The impact triggered the Safira's alarm.

"Drive, Jimmy, drive," shrieked Tyler.

I drove. I was crap. Not as good as on the karts. It was different. The car felt bigger than a petrol-powered 200cc Drifter go-kart. That's because it was. Why was I surprised at the time? I just didn't have the same control. Swerving all over the road, I bumped into parked cars.

But I was laughing. I was having the time of my life.

After a while, driving around Canterbury, sirens blared in the distance.

"You think those are for us?" said Tyler.

I said I didn't know.

"What should we do?" he said.

We dumped the car near the Kent and Canterbury Hospital. It was only a mile or so from where we'd nicked it, but it felt as if we'd driven for ages.

For days we were shitting ourselves. We waited for cops to arrive. The car was covered in out fingerprints.

But Brandon, Tyler's brother, said, "You ain't been done before so they don't have your records. Just don't get caught, that's all."

At the time I thought, *Okay, no problem.*

But it was easier said than done.

77

CHAPTER 21.
INTO THE CITY.

WE were screaming as we raced through the Westgate Towers. Instead of going right, following the A290, I went straight.

"What are you doing?" shrieked Tyler. "Go right, go right – "

I ignored him, although his voice was ringing in my ears. I thought my brain would explode.

Ahead of me lay St Peters Street. The cobbled street was crammed with people out for a Friday night. The clock in the car said 10.45 – a busy time in Canterbury.

Swerving round the traffic bollards, I sent three people diving into the kebab shop on the corner. More revellers turned our way, seeing what was coming.

And I could see in their faces the anger towards me turning to terror towards what was following me.

"You'll kill us," Tyler said, trying to grab me.

"Get off me," I shouted, shoving him away.

I looked quickly in the rear-view mirror. The chariot destroyed the Westgate arch.

"You see that?" I said.

Tyler had seen it and responded with even more screaming as the archway leading into the city erupted.

Although I'd never paid much attention at school, things did sink in. I had that kind of brain, and if I'd used it properly, I wouldn't have been driving like a nutter in a stolen car through Canterbury at that moment. But anyway, one thing that did filter through was that the Westgate Towers were built in the 1300s. So something that had stood for nearly 800 years had just been smashed to bits.

"Jesus, what are we supposed to do?" cried Tyler.

"I don't know, I don't know," I yelled back, racing down the road.

This was my fault. The destruction and the deaths. I was to blame.

Tyler was screaming his head off, trying to tell me where to go, saying, "Get us out of here, Jimmy, get us away."

The people in the street were screaming too. I could hear them. After all, they were in the path of an unstoppable force.

I drove like mad, the car bouncing and jerking all over the place.

"You've got to lose him," Tyler howled in my ear, as if I didn't know. As if the fear wasn't making me cold. As if my stomach wasn't churning. As if the sweat wasn't pouring off me. As if I was blind to all this.

I wished I was.

So I shut my eyes. Just for a second. A moment of peace. Then I opened them again.

And hell was still there, rampaging up the street.

I passed Nandos and pined for Sam. We had our first date there. We were kids. Nervous and making a mess with a whole chicken. Fingers greasy. T-shirt stained by Piri Piri sauce.

I drove on, wanting to cry, wanting Sam again.

Did the charioteer have her?

Drinkers piled out of a pub to see what was going on.

"Christ, look out," shouted Tyler.

Too late. I clipped a cab. The driver got out, waving his fist at me. I kept driving.

79

Behind me the driver disappeared in a ball of fire as the horses and the chariot ran him down.

Tyler was losing his mind: "Did you see that, oh shit, did you see that?"

"I saw it, I saw it – shut up," I told him, not doing a good job of holding on to my sanity.

Anything in the chariot's path was burned and crushed and tossed aside.

The horses' hooves ploughed up the street. The wheels gouged the pavements. People flung themselves into doorways, down alleyways, anywhere they could.

Unfortunately, not everyone made it.

They died under the wheels or under the horses' feet, burned, crushed, broken into pieces.

I'd take the fall for this. And maybe I should. No court would believe that a giant chariot pulled by enormous black horses had torn through Canterbury. There might be witnesses, but they wouldn't believe them.

But it had to be on CCTV, though. They surely wouldn't pin on me when they saw the footage.

Tears ran down my face. My eyes burned.

They would blame. I knew what courts were like.

I had a feeling they weren't going to catch whoever was chasing me, so I'd be the patsy.

I accelerated, determined to get away.

"Where are we going, where are we going?" yelled Tyler.

The car flew over the cobblestoned street.

"I don't know, shut your gob," I said.

I was causing chaos. I was driving for my life. I couldn't believe what was happening.

"Hold on," I said to Tyler.

"I am," he said, his voice a squeal.

I wrenched the steering wheel hard to the left.

Tyler screamed.

The car lifted up on two wheels.

It screeched around the corner into Best Lane.

Tyler and me were screaming.

In between screams he was saying, "What are you doing, you nutter? You're going to kill me."

The car was in danger of toppling over on its side.

I was thinking, *We're going over*, and if we did the charioteer would crush us.

But the Merc steadied again, bouncing as it came down on all four wheels.

I whooped. Tyler cried. "You're crazy," he whined.

I floored it down the narrow street, a quiet lane lined with town houses. Not quiet now, though.

The chariot turned to follow us. Its wheels scoured the buildings. The fire from them charred brickwork. Windows shattered. Doors flew off their hinges.

They've got insurance, I thought. But that was always my initial thought: *they've got insurance, so if I nick their car, or even break into their homes and nick a DVD player or laptop, they've got insurance.*

But now I realized that wasn't enough.

For the first time ever, I felt guilt.

Guilt for stealing people's possessions. Guilt for scarring lives.

I saw it in the doors smashing and the windows breaking.

I shook off my shame. I had to survive.

"Where are we going?" said Tyler in a panic. "Tell me where we're going."

"I don't know – anywhere – away from… from that thing behind us – anywhere – "

"Where, Jimmy? Where? Please don't let it catch us. I'm shitting myself."

I took a right down Orange Street. Another narrow road. Single lane. I hurtled down it, veering left and right, clipping the pavement.

The chariot came too. Storming down the road. Tearing it up. The quiet street now a ruin in its wake. Mock Tudor frontages burnt to cinder. White bricks blackened.

"It's still coming," cried Tyler. "You've got to lose the bastard."

"I'm trying, I'm trying."

I came out in a pedestrianized area packed with people. They were running out of the way. Panic had spread through the city now.

Four roads led off from the pedestrianized area.

I aimed right, down the narrow Sun Street.

The chariot followed. It ripped shops apart. Noa Noa drowned in fire.

"It's speeding up," said Tyler, "the bastard's speeding up."

I glanced at him. His face was red and tears ran down his cheeks. I'd never seen him so scared.

Then he shouted, "The cathedral."

On the left was the Cathedral Gate, a bronze figure of Jesus looking down at us.

My heart leapt.

Maybe, I thought, *if Satan exists, so does Jesus.*

I said a prayer, asking God or Jesus to save me from the devil chasing us. But I'm not sure if I believed – despite what my dad had told me before he died.

You entered the Cathedral precinct through this gate, but I didn't expect to see it open. It never was this late at night. But people were piling in, dozens of them as we charged up the road.

"Where are all those people going?" said Tyler.

I said nothing, just watched as the crowd shoved through the gate. They looked scared, and when they saw us, they started to hurry, pushing the people ahead of them.

They must have known we were coming. Known there was something terrible going on in Canterbury. Maybe the cathedral had opened up to give them sanctuary. Give them somewhere to hide from the devil.

I thought, *If anyone needed protecting from the devil, it's me.*

It was a stupid, cowardly thing I did, but when you're desperate, survival comes first.

I slammed my horn.

Tyler screamed, which was actually louder than the horn.

I turned left, slowing down, but keeping my hand on the horn.

"Shit, it's coming," said Tyler, looking over his shoulder.

I could tell. The night turned orange. The fire lighting the dark.

Tyler said, "What are you doing?"

The crowd shrieked and scattered. Some spilled through the gate into the cathedral precinct. Others, seeing what was coming up the road behind us, legged it down Burgate or Butchery Lane.

"Jimmy, where are you going?" yelled Tyler.

A man wearing a security guard's uniform tried to stop me going through the gates, but I swerved past him.

"You're mad," said Tyler.

"It's Christian, isn't it."

"You what?"

I drove side to side, trying to avoid the people running down, and then the road angled right.

The cathedral stood before us, lit up and enormous.

I shivered, and for a second everything was peaceful. Thoughts of Sammie filled my head. I thanked Jesus for saving us, and asked him to keep my girlfriend safe. For the first time I honestly thought everything was going to be okay.

"It's bloody coming," shrieked Tyler. "Put your foot down."

Behind us, the chariot crashed through the Cathedral Gate. Masonry shot from the shattered walls. People were running everywhere, trying to get away.

I headed up past the cathedral. I sensed that I was being watched, and I hoped it was someone kind, someone who could protect me.

I skidded along the lane, tires squealing.

"Here it comes," said Tyler, with his running commentary.

"I see, I see," I shouted.

I drove hard, the cathedral on my left.

The chariot followed, the horses tearing up the road.

Suddenly, my pursuer slowed down, and it got smaller and smaller in my rear-view mirror.

"What's it doing?" said Tyler.

I slowed down and watched.

"I don't know," I said.

The charioteer steered the horses so that they faced the cathedral. The animals reared up. The carriage driver cracked his whip, and it lashed towards the ancient building.

What looked like a tongue of fire shot from the whip. The tiny flame sailed through the darkness. It spattered against the front of the cathedral's walls and just died.

"What was that about?" said Tyler.

"I don't know, but I'm not hanging about to find – "

The earth trembled.

Tyler said, "What the – " but he never finished his sentence.

The cathedral started to crumble. Chunks of rubble tumbled from its roof. The walls started to crack. The windows shattered, and glass showered the ground. The bells started to clang, as if the building were crying for help. But it was too late. It was coming apart.

And Tyler and me just gawped, staring at this huge, ancient place turning to rubble, collapsing in front of us.

"We… we better go," said Tyler.

"W-why?"

"'Cause he's coming after us again."

I snapped out of my stare and looked over my shoulder.

The charioteer had me in his sights again.

I put my foot down.

By now the cathedral was disintegrating. The collapse sent clouds of dust everywhere. Soon it was like we were driving through fog. Tiny bits of rubble spattered the car. I had my wipers on, my headlights full beam, but I couldn't see where I was going.

"Do you know where we are?" said Tyler.

I said no.

"Do you know where you're going?"

No again.

The noise was incredible. The earth was shaking. The cathedral's destruction was like an earthquake.

"What did he do?" said Tyler. "What was that little flame? Did that make the place fall?"

"How do I know?"

I was driving blind. The chariot chased me. I saw grass in front of me. We were bouncing over a field now, churning up the soil. A building loomed out of the dust cloud.

"Look out," shouted Tyler.

"Oh, crap." I wrenched the steering wheel. The car lurched to the right. We tore through some bushes. The wheels grinded. I gritted my teeth.

"Don't break down, for Christ's sake," said Tyler.

"Shut up, Tyler. You're getting on my wick."

"I'm trying to help."

"Get out, then. That'll help."

"It's not my fault."

"You went behind my back with Sammie, so shut up."

We were going along a narrow lane between some tall buildings, the car scraping along, sparks flying.

Through the dust cloud behind me, the chariot appeared.

The horses' glowing, red eyes. The fiery wheels. The whip cracking.

I thought about that whip, the tiny tongue of flame that came from it and went out against the cathedral – before destroying the building.

Tyler was crying and shaking, shock probably hitting him now. I regretted saying what I'd said to him, but I was angry and scared. I wanted Sammie back. I didn't want to be here, being chased through dark, dust-filled alleyways by some creature from hell.

I floored the accelerator.

The car bucked and groaned.

The chariot trailed me. It destroyed everything that stood in its way. It had destroyed Canterbury Cathedral. A place that was supposed to be holy. A place where you were supposed to find God. A place lying in ruins.

I thought, *If Jesus and God can't stop this monster, how can I?*

CHAPTER 22.
OPENING THE BRIEFCASE.

I DON'T know how it happened, but we came out on Broad Street, which is behind the cathedral grounds.

A cloud of dust filled the sky. The remains of the cathedral floating up to God, I thought.

I drove down the road, around the city walls, and onto the A28.

Fires blazed in the city. Sirens blared. That cloud of ruins hung above us like a shroud.

"You've got to lose him, Jimmy," said Tyler, his teeth chattering.

I said nothing, just glanced in my rear-view mirror to see the chariot tearing around the corner after me.

As the A28 opened up into two carriageways, I made a decision.

I turned left and smashed through barriers into Church Street.

"Jimmy' it's a one-way – "

"When has that made any difference?" I said, screeching into Longport, past St Augustine's Abbey, straight on to the A257.

Behind me, there was empty road. The chariot had been snarled up in the narrow streets. The fire from its wheels rose up above the buildings. It was still coming, but it was out of sight.

I turned into the grounds of Barton Court Grammar School. Slowing down and switching off my headlights, I wended down the road and then stopped the car.

Everything was quiet except for my heartbeat and Tyler's whining.

There in the trees, we waited.

Whining and heartbeats.

Silence a wall around the whining and heartbeats.

Darkness everywhere.

Neither of us saying a word.

Too scared. Too confused. Too remorseful.

I could hear Tyler say, "I promise I'll behave... promise I'll behave," under his breath.

I glanced in the rear-view mirror, waiting.

Waiting for that terrible thing to wheel in through the school gates.

A rumble grew. I stiffened.

Tyler stopped whining and held his breath, staring at me.

"It... it's coming," he said.

I said nothing.

I waited.

I tensed.

In the rear-view mirror I saw fire turn the darkness orange. I held my breath.

The chariot swept past the entrance, a fiery ball of rage and anger. The whip cracked. The hooves thundered. The earth was ripped open.

And then it was gone, and the noise died away.

"He didn't see us, can you believe it?" said Tyler, and after a pause asked, "What is it, Jimmy, what the bloody hell is chasing us?"

I stayed quiet. I had no idea.

Sirens blared in the distance.

"Cops are on to them," said Tyler.

"Won't make a difference."

He was crying. "What have we done, Jimmy?"

I shook my head. "You left Sammie with… with that… "

"No… no, I didn't, I… "

"Shut up," I said and started the engine again so I could turn on the radio.

I tuned in the radio and quickly found someone talking about what was happening. A presenter was speaking in a panicky voice, reporting an earthquake in Kent.

"Earthquake?" said Tyler.

"I suppose they have to call it something."

"Why not call it what it is – something from hell, and it destroyed Canterbury."

"I don't know if they know that, yet."

"There were loads of witnesses, Jimmy."

"Most of them are dead."

"Jesus, what have we done?"

"We should've taken the car back."

"You heard what the… the man on the phone said – it didn't matter. It was too late. They're going to kill us, Jimmy, we're going to – "

"Shut up, Tyler. We've got to think. We've got to find them and get Sammie back."

His mouth fell open. "Find them? That's the opposite thing of what I want to do."

"It's what I want to do. You're a coward, Tyler. Always have been. You never stand up for your mates, ever."

"What d'you mean?"

"I mean you always leg it when there's trouble, leaving me to take the heat."

"No, I – "

"Yes you do. All the time. Mate? You? Bollocks."

"Come on, Jimmy."

"Come on, what? Your problem is, you learn everything from Brandon – you forget about everyone else, and just look after yourself."

89

He started crying again.

"You're useless," I said. "You should start standing up for things. For your friends. Your mates. And if you say you fancied Sammie, you should stand up for her. Help me find her, you useless git."

"I'm scared."

"You think I'm not scared? What did we just see? Do you know?"

He shook his head.

"No, me neither," I said. "I never saw anything like it. I never dreamed anything like it. My dad got... got his head cut off by a man with wings, Tyler. You think I'm not scared or confused? I am. But... but I still got to do the right thing, and the right thing is find Sammie."

I opened the car door.

"Where are you going?" he said

"To see what all the fuss is about."

I opened the boot. Tyler was next to me saying, "Don't leave me alone in the car. I'm shitting myself."

I ignored him. "Let's open one of these briefcases."

For a few seconds we both stared at the thirteen cases.

"Okay," I finally said, "this one," and I leaned into the boot. Licking my lips, I flicked open the clasps. They felt hot – so hot they burned my fingers. I flinched, ignoring the pain. "Ready, Tyler?"

He whined.

I opened the case. We both recoiled. The light was incredibly bright. It was golden and sprayed out of the case, lighting up everything around us.

I blinked over and over.

Tyler said, "What... what is it?"

"I can't see," I said.

90

I shielded my eyes. Slowly, my sight adjusted to the glare. I saw what was in the briefcase.

"It's… it's like one of those crystal ball things," said Tyler.

It was. A glass sphere sitting on a bed of red velvet. It was about the size of a cricket ball. Inside the sphere, floating around, was a golden light. It was very bright. Blindingly bright. It floated there like one of those lava lamps. My mum used to have one when I was really small. I remembered just staring at it all the time.

"What is it?" said Tyler again.

"I don't know."

"You… you think they're valuable?"

"Valuable enough to tear Canterbury apart. Valuable enough to kidnap Sammie – and kill my dad."

Fear crawled through me, making me shiver, making me hot.

I wished this were a dream. I wished I were at home with my dad watching Corrie, even if it meant not being with Sammie any more. I wished she were safe in her bedroom, angry with me, hating me, never wanting to see me again – but alive.

I wished, but that's all I did.

It meant nothing.

I stared at the golden orb.

I shut the case, and it was dark again.

"We've got to find Sammie and take these back," I said.

"Yeah, but what are they?" said Tyler.

I shut the boot, ready to tell him I had no idea what they were.

But I just froze and Tyler shrieked.

The winged man crouched on the roof of the car.

"They are souls," he said. "And you are thieves."

CHAPTER 23.
THE CHALLENGE.

"WIN," said the winged man, "and your dwarf here – "

"Dwarf?" said Tyler.

" – can live, and so can your pretty Samantha Louise Rayer," the winged man continued.

"Dwarf?" said Tyler again.

"Lose," said the winged man, "and they are doomed."

I looked him in the eye. They were black eyes. Like coal. His skin was pale and his hair black. His wings were wrapped against his back. He was naked, but he had no cock and balls. He had nothing down there. No cock, no cunt. Nothing. After having a good look, I stared at his face again.

"You didn't say what happens to me," I said.

"Oh, you're doomed whatever, Jimmy. Someone has to pay. I mean, you can give up one of the others if you like. The dwarf?"

Tyler squealed.

I stared at my friend. "You're not willing to die for me, then?" I asked him.

Tyler gawked and stumbled backwards. He looked terrified. I was terrified. I looked at the winged man again.

I said, "Why haven't you got any… " – I gestured towards his groin – "… equipment?"

He looked down at himself and laughed. "I'm an angel. We are neither male nor female. Only the creatures on this earth are male or female."

"Not... not all of them," said Tyler. "There's... there's worms and they're... they're herma-hermaphrodites, they... "

"How the hell d'you know that?" I said.

The winged man shrugged. "I'm not here to talk about things that crawl. I'm here to give you hope. Give you a chance. I could easily take back what you've stolen from us. But my master, he's a considerate individual. He wants to give you a chance."

"I'm going to die either way," I said.

"Yes, but your dwarf isn't, and neither is Samantha."

"Don't call me a dwarf again," said Tyler.

The winged man turned to look at him and then spread his wings. They were huge – about fifteen feet from tip to tip. He flapped them gently and they brushed the air.

Then he slashed them and they produced a gust of wind that tossed Tyler through the air.

My mate screamed and crashed into the trees.

"You hurt him," I said.

"Hurt? You have no idea about hurt, Jimmy. You will know hurt, be sure of that. The hurt that is coming to you is beyond everything you have suffered. It will out do all your previous agonies. And if you don't win the race, this will also be Samantha's fate. And Tyler's. If you want to know pain, ask your father."

My blood boiled.

The angel laughed. "I enjoyed killing him. His soul went straight to hell. He was just too late for salvation. I sensed he was about to ask for redemption, but like so many who face their doom, he ran out of time."

I tried to calm down, let the anger seep out me.

By then Tyler had staggered back towards us, groaning and complaining.

"Okay," I said to the angel. "Tell me about the race."

"The race is easy. There's a place not to far from here. Abandoned. Derelict. Forgotten. We'll use that. My master is looking forward."

"Is... is your master the devil?"

He smiled. "He has many names."

"So... what are the rules of this race?"

"The rules are you finish first, then Samantha and Tyler go free. We take back what's ours – the souls which you stole – and we take you to hell – where you will roast for eternity."

It all felt like a nightmare.

I looked at the car. "Whose souls are they?"

"My master's."

"No, before."

The winged man shrugged. "Thirteen of the thousands who make a deal with him. They crave success, greatness, and they crave women, men. Some crave far worse things. But a deal is a deal. Would you sell your soul?"

"I'd sell it for Sammie."

"And that's what you are doing. Are you ready?"

I said nothing.

"Are you, Jimmy?"

"Who am I racing against?"

"You've met them before."

I heard them before I saw them. The horses neighed and snorted, their hooves pounding the earth, the noise becoming louder.

Here it came – the chariot, roaring across the fields, ploughing them with its fiery wheels.

Tyler said "No... no, not again... "

A black Ford Galaxy raced down the road, its headlights blinding me.

The people carrier stopped near us and two men leapt out. The men were hefty. They wore dark suits and sunglasses. They came straight for Tyler. He started to leg it. I stiffened with fear. The men grabbed him and carried him towards the vehicle.

I said to the angel, "What are you doing?"

"Don't fret, Jimmy, he's just being taken to his front-row seat, that's all. You'll see him again – if you win. Now, are you ready?"

I watched the Galaxy drive off. Its windows were tinted, but I knew Tyler was there, his face pressed against them, his hands clawing for a way out.

I said, "First, I want to see my dad."

The angel smiled. "If you must. But he's not a pretty sight."

CHAPTER 23.
SEEING SAMMIE.

12.02AM, JUNE 4, 2011

I STILL had tears on my face after seeing my dad – or what my dad was now.

But I put what I saw and heard out of my mind. I was going to race.

To be a racing driver was my dream. To challenge other drivers. To beat them.

When I was racing those go-karts a few years back, it had been fun. Winning was easy. I hated coming second or third, and it hurt. But I never actually lost anything except for the race – and my pride.

But this was serious. If I lost this race, something would be gone forever – something more precious than my pride.

I was racing for Sammie's life.

We were on waste ground. In the distance, the lights of Canterbury glimmered. Fire stained the sky above the city. The cloud of dust from the collapsed cathedral still hung over the area. Helicopters wheeled, casting their spotlights into the ruined streets.

I wondered how many had died.

All down to me.

All down to my spineless decision to steal this car.

Guilt welled up in my chest. I wanted the ground to open up and swallow me.

And then I remembered that if I lost this race, it would do just that.

And once under the earth, I'd burn.

That's what the angel had said – and what my dad had told me.

How could my dad be in hell? He wasn't a bad man. I'd thought only bad men went to hell. Wasn't that how it worked? I know I was bad, and if I'd thought about it, I'd be headed to hell. But it's not something you think about when you're seventeen. You're immortal. Death's a long way away. Most times it is. But sometimes, like now, it's right in your face.

The angel had led us deep into the countryside.

The waste ground was littered with burnt-out cars. A derelict multi-storey car park stood at the centre on the land. It was a slab of ugly concrete, stained black by time and the elements.

It looked out of place here in the middle of rural Kent. Graffiti covered building, the language of the words strange to me. Then I remembered the writing on the briefcases. The letters scrawled on the building looked similar to the ones carved on the cases. Thinking about it sent a shiver down my spine, though I didn't know why.

"What is this place?" I said.

"A playground," the angel said.

I knew we were somewhere off Bekesbourne Lane, a single track road I'd often raced down. The area was rural. I knew it reasonably well, though my travels in the area had taken place at high speeds with a cop car on my tail. Not much time for taking in the scenery, so I must have missed this place.

"I never seen it before," I said.

"There are many places you've not seen before, Jimmy," said the angel.

I glared at him. If I could, I would've attacked him. He'd killed my dad. But I knew it would be pointless. He was stronger than me. He'd rip me apart. I had to be patient.

"Where's Sammie?" I said.

The Ford Galaxy crawled out of the multi-storey's exit.

The car stopped about twenty yards away, and the two blokes I'd seen earlier came out.

Something came to my head. "What happened to the guys we saw putting the briefcases in the car outside your house?"

"Those two fools?" said the angel. "They were punished."

I didn't need to know any more than that.

One of the big blokes opened the back door of the people carrier. I heard her before I saw her, and my heart leapt.

The man pulled Sammie out, and she was kicking and screaming.

My stomach lurched. Love for her filled my chest. Fear for her sapped my bowels.

She shouted my name and tried to get to me, but the man held her. She was crying and saying, "What's going on, what's going on?"

"It'll be okay, Sammie," I yelled.

"Jesus," she said, seeing the man with wings. "What's that? Jimmy, what's happening? Oh, please. That little bastard, Tyler, he – "

Tyler, I thought. *Where was he?*

Anger rose up in me.

Sod him.

If it weren't for him, I wouldn't be in this situation. My dad would be alive. Sammie would be safe. But then, looking at Sammie, I knew it wasn't Tyler's fault. It was pointless blaming other people. I was to blame. I'd had choices. I made the wrong ones.

And here I was, with the angel of death on waste land in the middle of nowhere.

"Are you okay?" I asked Sammie.

"What's going on, Jimmy?"

"It's okay, I'll sort it out."

The man with wings laughed.

Sammie said, "Why's he got wings?"

"Don't think about it, babe," I told her.

"What have you done, Jimmy?" she said.

"Nothing," I said.

"Is it Tyler? Has he got mixed up with something bad and dragged you along?"

"No," I said. "It's okay."

"Put her in the car," said the angel.

After the men locked her in the Galaxy again, the angel turned to me and said, "Are you ready to race for her life?"

"Where's Tyler?" I asked as the Galaxy drove back into the multi-storey.

"You'll find him. Your opponent is waiting."

He pointed at the car lot. From around the corner, the chariot appeared. The horses snorting. The driver looming.

"You will race to the top level," said the angel, "picking up your friends on the way. They are there, waiting. You pick them up, or he will pick them up. First out with the two humans wins."

"What if I get one human?" I asked, thinking I'd leave Tyler in there, get out with Sammie.

"You lose," said the angel.

There goes that plan, I thought.

The Galaxy drove out of the multi-storey again.

"Are you ready?" said the angel.

"You want to take the briefcases out of the car before I thrash it around that place?"

He smiled. "No, they can stay in the vehicle."

"They'll get damaged."

"Well that would be too bad, Jimmy. You see, even if you win the race, you will lose if any of those precious items are damaged. Samantha and Tyler are ours if there's a scratch on those treasures – and they do scratch easily, Jimmy."

I looked him in the eye and said, "You shit."

He flapped his wings. "You think this is going to be fair? You don't realize what you've done. You are an insect, Jimmy. You could be easily crushed. But my master, he likes a wager. And he likes the cut of your soul, young fellow. He's intent on winning it for his collection."

He beckoned to the Galaxy. One of the blokes stepped out, carrying a briefcase.

My balls shrivelled.

He handed the briefcase to the angel, who opened it. Its velvet interior had a spherical shape cut into it. One of those golden orbs would fit perfectly into the shape.

I had a bad feeling, which started in my chest and seeped right the way down into my legs.

"A carriage for your soul, Jimmy," said the angel.

CHAPTER 24.
THE RACE.

I SAT behind the wheel of the stolen Mercedes, thirteen hell-bound souls in the boot.

Two more souls lay in the darkness of the multi-storeyed car park. Two souls I had to save, or they'd be in briefcases bound for hell too – just like me.

Sadness filled my heart. I was doomed. I had no choice but to die. I had no choice but to save Sammie, and Tyler too.

I thought about my dad.

I'd never talked to him when he was living, but when he was dead we'd suddenly become close. Had a real chat.

I was still convinced this was a dream, but it was getting to be very, very real.

The radio in the Merc was still on. I turned up the volume.

Reports of death and carnage in Canterbury came over the airwaves. Dread laced the reporter's voice. Sounds of devastation mingled with his shaky, nervous voice. He was obviously in Canterbury somewhere, reporting from the scene. You could hear sirens and screams. You could hear death and destruction. A city built for God, destroyed by the Devil.

"Are you ready?" said the winged man.

I glanced across at the chariot. Fire smouldered on its wheels. The horses strained at the reins. The charioteer waited, whip loose by his side.

I said, "Yes, I'm – "

The chariot shot off into the car park, leaving a trail of fire behind it.

The winged man laughed.

I floored the accelerator, getting right up the chariot's arse.

The driver looked at me over his shoulder. There was just a black space where his face should be. Just darkness in that hood.

He snapped his whip towards me. Instinctively I ducked. The whip lashed my windscreen. A crack appeared.

The car swerved. The chariot pulled away.

I swore and speeded up, following the carriage into the empty car lot.

My headlights and the chariot's fiery wheels lit up the gloom. Pillars cast shadows as we raced along the first level. I had to be careful not to plough into one of them, because they reared up suddenly out of the dark.

I looked around, seeing if I could spot Tyler or Sammie.

What had the angel done to them?

Where could they be?

The chariot tore through the car park, heading for the ramp in the far left corner. Its wheels chewed up the tarmac.

I swerved side to side, trying to avoid the newly-gouged potholes.

I came level with the chariot now and looked up at the driver.

He leaned forward over his horses, cracking the whip and then glanced at me.

In the darkness of his face, I saw hate and agony.

It made me lose my concentration for a second.

And when he lurched left towards me, I shouted in terror.

The chariot rammed the Merc.

I lost control and swung left.

Metal creaked as the chariot sheared along the side of the car. Sparks flew. Fire filled my window. I felt the heat, and it made me pull away, driving off to the side to escape the fire.

The chariot headed for the ramp.

I sped up, trying to catch up, but my opponent had a good lead. Sweat broke out on my back.

The chariot shot up the ramp, carving it up.

I cursed.

The chariot swung around the corner, up towards the next level. The glow of its fiery trail illuminated the wall ahead of me, which seemed to be covered in paintings of a burning city.

Although I only got a quick glimpse of the mural, I recognized a landmark shown in it immediately. It was Canterbury Cathedral. The town was Canterbury. And it was burning to the ground, its people trapped in a hell on earth.

I swallowed, my throat dry. My insides felt liquidy and cold.

The Merc hit the rutted ramp. It jerked and bucked. I was tossed around. I had to slow down, or the suspension would be shot. I crawled up the ramp, took the corner, and then speeded up. The engine groaned. The gears clanked. The car jolted. But I got up the ramp and entered Level 2 of the car park.

The chariot was up ahead.

I went down a gear and revved the engine hard.

The Merc picked up speed. The engine complained, whining as I pushed it to its limit.

But I was gaining on my opponent.

I slammed the gear stock into top.

The car accelerated and I came up to the chariot and clipped its rear wheel. Fire spat across my windscreen.

The chariot swerved to the side, allowing me to stretch ahead.

I could see the exit up to the next ramp.

I had it in my sights – for a second.

Then I saw there was something blocking the ramp – something tied across it.

Something or someone.

I went cold.

My headlights illuminated the ramp and I saw the obstacle.

It was Tyler.

He was tied between two pillars, ropes attached to his arms. He kicked and writhed, trying to get loose. His face was twisted with fear.

I knew the way he'd been secured that the chariot would drive straight over him. There was no way those horses would stop. Anyway, they wanted Tyler dead – they wanted his soul.

And they wanted Sammie's soul too.

CHAPTER 25.
PLAN.

ONCE more I accelerated. The Merc felt heavy in my hands. I thought I was going to lose control of it. But I tightened my muscles, tensed every nerve, gritted my teeth.

I had to get in front of the chariot so I could rescue Tyler. I couldn't bump the thing out of the way – it had torn through a train in Canterbury, and ripped down ancient walls.

I'd lose a battle of strength with it.

The car, and me, would get smashed.

And then Tyler and Sammie would be doomed.

I tried to think as I accelerated and pulled away. I glanced in the rear-view mirror. I had a ten-yard lead.

Not enough of an advantage to stop the car, jump out, rescue Tyler, get back in, and drive off before the chariot's wheels ripped me and the Merc, and everything inside to bits.

I thought of something.

I sat up in my seat, excited.

I had a plan, a tiny speck of one, but still better than nothing. Better than hoping for the best and better than praying.

I drove straight towards Tyler. He was thrashing about. I had a good head start on the chariot, with its wheels spitting fire as it tried to catch up.

When I was fifty yards from Tyler, I took one quick look behind me and made a decision.

Now, I thought.

I slammed on the brakes.

The tires screeched and the car came to a halt.

The chariot closed on me, vast and black and fiery.

My heart nearly split.

For a moment I thought my plan had gone pear-shaped.

I nearly rammed the car back into gear and got going again, this time without a scheme.

But just as I thought the chariot would plough into me, the horses reared back. I gawped as the lifted up into the air, pulling the chariot with them. They climbed over the car. The chariot's wheels scraped the Merc's roof. The horses shrieked, flailing wildly, whirling around.

I sped away, looking in the side mirror.

The chariot wheeled in the air, its driver trying to control the frantic horses, the wheels spinning, throwing flames everywhere.

My gamble had paid off.

I got to Tyler and put the car into neutral, before leaping out. He was screaming and shouting at me. I untied him. He made a run for it but I grabbbed him and said, "Get in the car, we're finding Sammie."

He was crying. I opened the back door and shoved him in.

He screamed, "It's coming, it's coming!"

And it was. Full pelt. Angrier and more fiery than ever. I could feel the hate emanating from the horses and the driver. The hate at being cheated, at being tricked.

I revved hard, the car shrieking up the ramp towards Level 3.

Adrenaline coursed through me. I had the edge. I knew how to beat him.

"Why did you stop like that, you nut?" said Tyler. "I thought we were mash, that he was going to crush us."

"He's not going to destroy this car."

"Why? It's only a car."

"What's in the boot, Tyler?"

I glanced at him in my rear-view. He opened his mouth but said nothing.

"There's no way that thing, whatever it is," I said, "will destroy this car while those souls are in the back."

I'd remembered what the angel had told me – any damage to the cargo, and I was dead for sure. He'd left the briefcases in the boot to make sure I drove carefully and slowly. He didn't want me to stand any chance of beating the chariot.

I'd been driving like a nut anyway. There was no way I'd let them win. The souls might well have been damaged. But I had to take that risk.

My mind was going round and round at that time, trying to come up with a way out for Sammie, Tyler, and me. First, I had to win the race. And I'd do that even if I had to cheat.

Tyler started whimpering: "I… I don't know what I would have done without you, Jimmy."

"What are you talking about?"

"I… I… I don't think I would have had the guts to come looking for you like you did for me. I just don't think… "

"Don't worry about it, mate," I said. "Let's get out of here first, then you can think of millions of ways to make it up to me."

I said that, but knew it wasn't going to happen – my soul was the devil's.

"I'm really sorry for being a useless friend," he said.

"Forget it," I said.

And then the chariot roared around the corner, ripping away concrete and steel, and I accelerated up the ramp, overshooting, the car leaving the ground, and coming down hard on the flat.

CHAPTER 26.
THE SEARCH FOR SAM.

I HAD an advantage, and I wasn't going to let it go.

In a race, if you get to the front, you need to stay there.

The ramp leading up to the fourth level lay on the far side of the parking ground. I fixed my gaze on the number 4 painted in red on the off-white wall.

It was my finishing line. My chequered flag.

Sweat poured off me. My teeth hurt because I was grinding them so much. I could smell fire and rubber and petrol.

In my rear-view mirror, I could always see the glimmer of orange from the flames shooting off the chariot – a constant reminder of what was chasing me.

In the back seat, Tyler cried. He'd been crying a lot in the past few hours. Maybe he was changing. We were both changing.

If I got out of this, my bad ways would be behind me. Sammie was my future. But I knew that win or lose this race, the angel of death had said I had no future.

Dread filled me. But I had to ignore the terror for now. Hold it at bay so I could find Sammie and get her out of here.

I drove hard towards the ramp, determined to win, determined to rescue my girl.

The horses galloped after me.

Tarmac smashed under their hooves.

The chariot's wheels furrowed the asphalt.

I made it to the ramp and shot up it, the car bouncing. I came out into Level 4 and skidded, the back of the Merc swinging out.

"Look out for Sammie," I said to Tyler.

"Where is she?"

"How should I know?"

"I'm sorry about everything."

"Just look for Sammie."

Behind me, the chariot tore up the ramp, scything away the walls.

My gaze flickered all around the fourth level.

"Can you see anything?" I said.

"Just… no… it's scary… those pillars… oh, shit, he's coming… "

I heard him. The horses shrieked. The whip cracked. He'd closed on me again, pulling out to overtake.

He wouldn't try to ram me. Not with the souls in the boot. But he was going to try to win the race. Then me and my friends would be done for.

I pulled away again, dropping down through the gears, hammering the engine, revving hard, shifting from third to fourth to top gear.

The pillars seemed to be giant bollards. I weaved around them. Weirdly I was enjoying this – or part of me was.

It was a race, and that's what I always wanted to do.

I wanted to race for money, for glory.

But I'd found myself racing for my life, and for the lives of my friends.

That's pressure.

A feeling of hopelessness filled my chest.

What if Sammie wasn't here?

She was nowhere to be seen on this level.

Maybe the winged man had already taken her to hell.

I watched my pursuer gain on me.

For a moment I felt completely lost. Maybe this was all a game. I convinced myself that they'd already taken Sammie away, and all this was just pointless.

I couldn't trust these creatures. They were worse than criminals. Worse than me and Tyler.

I kept going, driving towards the next level. What did I have to lose? My life was over anyway.

I pulled away, weaving between the pillars, heading for the fifth level.

My heart thundered. I felt light-headed.

Sammie would be here. She had to be there. There was no room for doubt or fear or uncertainty.

I had to believe.

I had to have faith.

I would definitely see her again and save her life – but would it be enough to save her soul?

CHAPTER 27.
LEVEL 5.

I SPOTTED Sammie the moment I drove up the ramp and entered Level 5.

"She's over there," I said, barely able to get the words out.

They'd tied by her arms her between two pillars on the wall of the multi-storey car park. She was stretched out, her feet just touching the top of the wall. Behind her, the sky had gone pitch black. It was deep night. I could see her clearly against the darkness – she was blonde and wore white, looking to me like an angel. My angel. The angel I'd lost. And now I was getting her back.

"He's coming up behind us," shouted Tyler, snapping me out of my stare. "And he's coming quickly."

I needed a decent lead on my pursuer. I was going to have to stop, jump out, release Sammie, chuck her in the car, and get going again before the charioteer caught up.

Just like I'd done with Tyler.

I knew I had the edge, and I felt confident.

I ignored my pursuer and focused on Sammie.

This was my night. I was going to win the race – the most important race of my life.

Adrenaline punched my heart. I found more acceleration somewhere. Opening up a lead on the chariot, I started to feel relaxed and strong.

I said, "I'm stopping right there, then getting Sammie – you stay in the car."

"But he'll run me down – "

"No he won't – not with the briefcases in the back."

I wheeled the car round, burning rubber, facing the chariot.

I leapt out.

Sammie shouted my name. She hung there on the ledge, arms bound.

The chariot hurtled towards us, tearing across the parking area, weaving around the pillars.

"I thought you'd never come," she said, and my heart melted.

"I'll always come to get you," I told her, tearing at the ropes, undoing the knots, my fingers bleeding.

I pulled her off the ledge and shoved her in the car before getting in myself.

The horses roared, smoke billowing from their nostrils.

The charioteer lashed his whip.

I sped off, heading straight for the carriage.

Sammie screamed.

Tyler said, "What are you doing?"

"Playing chicken with an angel of death," I said.

The demon would do anything to avoid the Merc – I was convinced.

And I was right.

At the last second, with Sammie and Tyler screaming their heads off, the chariot swerved out of my path.

Fire splashed across the windscreen. It was like being in an oven. I drove through the flames and headed for the exit ramp.

I laughed.

Sammie told me I was crazy.

Tyler shrieked.

"We're okay," I said. "We're away."

"He's still coming," said Tyler.

I glanced in the side mirror. The chariot ploughed after me.

"I've got a head start. No way will it catch me. No way."

I was now thinking of how all three of us would escape. I'd already won a reprieve for Sammie and Tyler. Now I wanted to live as well.

I heard a rumble, and the ground trembled beneath us, making the car shudder.

A cracking noise filled the air.

The trembling increased, the ground quaking now, the car swerving all over the place.

Sammie said, "What's that?"

Tyler said, "Oh shit – drive quicker, drive quicker."

I said, "What's the – "

I slowed and turned the car to the right so I could see out of my side window.

The chariot came at me.

I gawped. Fear made me cold.

Instead of weaving around the pillars, the horses ploughed straight through them, and the chariot followed, smashing the concrete to smithereens.

The pillars crumpled, and with them came the ceiling, falling down in big chunks. The ground cracked again. A fissure appeared in the tarmac, and it was coming straight towards us.

The whole place was collapsing.

"Drive!" came the scream, and I had no idea if it was Sammie or Tyler, but I slammed the car into gear and raced away just as the ground split.

CHAPTER 28.
COLLAPSE.

AS we reached the exit ramp on the fourth level, the whole floor collapsed, just like the fifth had done.

The parking lot was caving in.

And through the falling masonry came the charioteer.

The rubble rained down, crashing to the ground seconds behind the car. Bits of debris showered the roof of the car. Dust coated the windscreen.

I was sweating. Tyler and Sammie were screaming.

Behind us, the horses' eyes glowed red in the storm of falling mortar.

"Go quicker," said Tyler.

The car made strange noises – clanking, growling, screeching. Its suspension creaked. The engine coughed. It had taken a battering.

And it took another one as I flung it down the ramp, swinging it around the corner, not caring now if I clipped a wing or cracked a bumper.

I didn't care that the contents of the boot could be getting damaged. I had no intention of playing by the rules. The briefcases could well be dented or scratched, which meant Tyler and Sammie were dead despite me winning the race. And there was no way I was stopping so the angel could announce me as the winner – and then take us all to hell.

We skidded around the corner, down into the third level.

"Look at that," said Sammie.

She was pointing at the ceiling, which was already giving way under the pressure from the collapsed fourth and fifth floors.

The pillars were buckling. The noise of the collapse was immense – a roaring, as if a huge animal was trapped in the structure.

I was driving fast, ramming through the gears. Rubble rained down. Dust filled the air. The whole world seemed to quake. The ground cracked. Everything was coming apart, falling to pieces.

I raced as hard as I could. Blisters formed on my fingers because I was gripping the wheel so tightly. My lips bled where I bit them. Everything hurt.

I glanced in the rear-view mirror. Down the ramp came the horses, steam rising from their glistening bodies.

I hit the ramp leading down to Level 2, and the car lifted off the ground. We smacked the concrete hard as we landed.

My head snapped back. For a few seconds, my vision was blurred. I had a pain in my neck. The Merc clipped the wall. Metal scraped on concrete. Sparks flew. The car weaved wildly from side to side. Sammie screamed.

"He's gaining on us," said Tyler.

I got the car under control again and shot down the ramp and out into the parking area.

As we sped across the second level, the ceiling bowed, the weight of the collapsing building pressing down on it.

"That's going to give any second," I said.

And it started to – cracks appearing, chunks of concrete exploding around us, peppering the car with shrapnel.

I zigzagged around the missiles.

All across the parking area, the pillars crumpled.

"Here he comes," said Tyler, confirming the charioteer was again on my tail.

I was nearly at the ramp leading to the first level. All I had to do then was drive like mad through the exit, out into the wasteland.

They'd be waiting for us. The angel and those thugs.

Tears came to my eyes. I felt hopeless.

I glanced at Sammie. She was beautiful, even now. Hair all messy. Eye make-up stained. Face paled by dread. Still beautiful.

I made it to the exit ramp on Level 2, the building coming down around me. As I hurtled down the slope, the walls around me started to crack. Shards of cement shot from them like bullets as the pressure came from above.

The car bounced down into Level 1.

Panic hit me like a hammer.

"The gates are shut – they've shut the gates," said Sammie, her voice a high-pitched squeal.

"You bastards," I said.

They'd locked us in. They weren't even going to give us a chance to escape. We would be crushed.

I looked at the gates. Moonlight splintered through the slats. I could drive into them, but the car would be a write-off, and we'd be trapped in the wreckage.

But I had no choice.

"I've got to keep driving," I said. "I can't stop here. The building's collapsing."

"And that bastard is still chasing us, too," said Tyler.

I headed straight for the gate.

"What are you doing?" said Sammie.

"I don't know."

"You'll kill us," she said.

"We're dying anyway, if this building falls on top of us."

She looked over her shoulder. In my mirror I saw what she was seeing. The roof caving in. The pillars toppling. The chariot surging across the parking area, smashing through them.

"Let me out; I'll open the gate," said Tyler.

"You what?" I said.

"Let me out, Jimmy."

"No way. You won't have time to get back in the car."

"Let me out, I'll be okay – I'm… I'm fast."

I looked at him in the rear-view mirror. He wasn't fast. He was podgy. But he had a steely look on his face, although his eyes were full of tears. I'd never seen him look so determined.

"I can't," I said.

"Do it, Jimmy," he said. "Or we'll all die."

"Do something," said Sammie.

We were fifty feet from the gate.

I slammed on the brakes.

The tires screeched. Smoke poured from them. Burning rubber made me dizzy, and it blew up a cloud, which gave us cover.

The chariot was lost in the smoke.

"Hurry," I told Tyler as he leapt out of the car, "and I'll wait for you."

I crawled after him.

The chariot shot out of the cloud.

"Oh, it's really close, Jimmy," said Sammie.

I said nothing, just watched Tyler crank open the gate. It started to open, slowly.

I slammed the accelerator. The car jerked over a speed bump and through the gate, just as Jimmy finished opening it.

The winged man appeared in front of me, and the two thugs leapt out of the ford Galaxy.

I stopped and waited for Tyler.

Sammie leaned out of the window and shouted at him, "Come on, Tyler."

I looked for him in my side-mirror and saw him, and my blood froze. "No, Tyler," I said. "No, don't – "

He was shutting the gate. He was still inside.

"Go, go," he shouted. "Just go."

117

The winged man launched himself towards us. The thugs came running.

"Go," Tyler screamed.

"Oh, God, the building… " said Sammie.

Just as Tyler shut the gate, on himself and the chariot, the multi-storey collapsed.

I cried out, desperate to save Tyler. I nearly leapt out of the car and ran towards the ruin.

But I knew there was no hope.

I floored the accelerator, clipping the winged man, sending him spiralling through the air.

One last glance in my rear view mirror – Jimmy's red hoodie standing out in the dust and debris and then gone as the car park fell into a pile of rubble, crushing him and the chariot.

A cloud of thick, grey dust spread out across the waste ground, rolling after us like a wave.

I saw it coming. The angel got lost in it as did his thugs, drowned in the dense mist of cement and brick dust.

I drove like mad, screaming and crying, Sammie screaming and crying next to me.

The cloud enveloped everything.

I hit the road and drove, not knowing where I was going. The mist of masonry kept coming, but the further we got from the wasteland, the thinner it got until finally we left it, just a few particles floating in the air.

Behind us in the distance, the horizon flared.

A fire somewhere.

A city burning.

Canterbury ablaze.

CHAPTER 29.
IT'S ALL ABOUT FAITH.

EARLIER that night at Barton Court Grammar School, my dead dad had told me what my chances were. Not good. But then he was always optimistic – not. He never had much hope for my future. But he loved me, I knew that now. Over the years he had always had my back. It seemed like he didn't care. But if you put all the little things he did for me together, they made one big pile. He was at it all the time, throughout my teenage years.

He'd covered for me. He'd fibbed for me. He'd died for me.

The angel had agreed to my demand to see me dad before I raced the devil's henchman. He told me, "Over there, then. Wait for his ghost," and I went into the trees.

In the distance sirens screamed. Canterbury in ruins. The 999 switchboards must have been overloaded. And I'd caused it. Me and the devil.

A heavy feeling filled my chest. I mourned the city. I mourned my dad. I waited for him in the woods.

"Hello, son."

I wheeled. For a second I was frozen with fear.

He came through the trees as if they weren't there. He was as white as snow, apart from his red eyes.

I backed up when he got close.

He saw my fear and said, "I'm still your dad."

I looked him up and down. A black line ran horizontally across his throat.

"Where he cut my head off," he said.

I was trying to keep myself together, trying not to tremble and piss myself.

He went on, "They say you're at peace when you die. That's what they told me about your mum. But it's not true. It's just a long, terrible wait. Eternity is long. Just depends where you're waiting, that's all."

"Are you… where… " I tripped over my words. I wanted to ask –

"Hell," he said, answering my question.

I didn't know what to say.

"It's not just evil people who go there, Jimmy. It's the unsaved. I was nearly saved. Nearly put my faith in… you know. It was up at the allotment. Before that bastard got me. Never mind."

What did he mean? I didn't understand. I shook off my confusion and said, "I've got souls in the back of the car."

I thought Dad could help me. He'd done it in life, I'd realized, so maybe he could also do it in death

But he shook his head. "You stole the devil's possessions, Jimmy."

"I… I didn't know."

"It doesn't wash in court. It doesn't wash in hell."

"I've really messed up this time."

"I tried to tell you."

I looked at the ground. "You should never have covered for me, Dad. All those times you lied for me, giving me alibis, saying I was somewhere else. All those times… maybe we wouldn't be here, now. Maybe you wouldn't be… "

"So it's my fault?"

"No, I don't mean that. It was my fault. But I couldn't see it. You should've taught me a lesson."

I was sure there were tears in those blazing red eyes. "But I love you son," he said, "like I loved you then. You were my little boy, and I wanted you to be safe. I was weak, I know. I should have been harder on you. Your mum would've been harder."

"Dad... "

"What?"

"Is Mum... "

"She's with me."

I creased my brow. "Mum in hell? But she was good, wasn't she?"

"I told you, it's not about being good – it's about being saved."

"How do you get saved?"

"Put your faith in Jesus, they tell me. Just faith."

"I thought Mum believed in Jesus."

"Faith and belief are different things, son."

"But I don't have to be good?"

"Well, once you put your faith in him, you're expected to behave like he'd behave, but... " He shrugged. "Some people do nasty things and still end up in heaven. Who are we to question?"

I said nothing. That was all in the future. Kids my age don't care much for the years ahead. We live in the now, in the moment.

And the moment for me was survival.

"How do I get out of this, Dad?"

"What's he told you?"

I explained. How if I won the race, Sammie and Tyler would go free. How the angel would take the souls back. How I'd be dead, whatever the result of the race.

My dad sighed. "It would be nice to have company."

"Uh... "

"But it wouldn't matter whether you'd be down there or not. Your mum is, and I don't see her. We see no one. Part of the punishment. Solitude is the suffering here. For most of us. Being alone hurts so much. When I was alive, I had Corrie, my allotment – down there – nothing."

He blew air out of his cheeks and looked me in the eye.

"Don't trust him, Jimmy," he said. "He won't keep his side of the bargain. But he'll expect you to keep yours. You can't beat him, but you can trick him. You've got to be at your best, son. There is a way. I don't know if it'll save your life, but it might save your soul."

I listened.

After he told me he said, "I'd love to hug you. I should've done more of that when I was alive. But I can't. I have to go. I love you, Jimmy. Always did. You have to know that."

"I know," I said and I was crying.

"Remember, son – faith. Always have faith… "

My dad's spirit faded, and then there was nothing but the night and the trees, and me crying among them.

CHAPTER 30.
MAKE OFFERINGS.

1.32AM, JUNE 4, 2011

"ARE we safe, Jimmy?" Sammie asked.

We were on the A257, just driven through Peddling Hill and heading towards Ash. It was a quiet road, flanked by tall bushes. I kept glancing in the rear-view mirror. No one followed us. But I did see an orange glow in the sky over Canterbury.

The city was dead.

I shivered. Even if we got through this, where would we go? Our homes would be gone. Nothing would be the same.

I answered Sammie. "I don't know."

"Oh... I need you to tell me it's okay."

I said nothing.

I kept driving.

"Is it going to be okay, Jimmy?"

"I don't know," I said again.

She wept. "What's happening? What's going on?"

"Why did you go out with Tyler?"

My gaze was fixed on the road ahead. It was dark, not much traffic. We were alone. It felt like we were the only people left on earth.

"I didn't," she said. "He told me... he told me you wanted to see me, and did I want to come in his car."

"He told you that?"

"Yes. Did you want to see me?"

"Of course I did, but not like that. I never said that to Tyler. He told me he was pulling some bird with it."

I turned right down the Ash road and stopped in a layby.

I listened to the silence for a moment before looking at Sammie, and she looked back at me.

She was so gorgeous. My heart felt like it was melting. Grief swelled up in me. I might not see her again after tonight. I'd give anything for things to be normal again. I'd change my whole life for her if I could. Easy to say that now, though, with the world falling apart. Shame I hadn't done it years back when I had the chance.

"Tyler said I wanted to see you," I said, "and… and you went with him?"

She blushed. "Of course."

"But I'd been trying to get in touch with you all day, and you just ignored me."

"I was pissed off."

"I know."

"And I wanted to… to make you feel like I'd felt when you broke all those promises."

"Okay. You did. Can we be friends again?"

She nodded. We kissed. It made everything bright and soft in my heart. It blew away the shadows and darkness and the evil for a few second.

"And you never fancied Tyler?"

"No, Jimmy. No way. Poor Tyler. He was really brave back there. He was usually just stupid and gutless, but he was really brave."

"He was. I can't believe he's gone. My dad too."

She hugged me. I cried into her shoulder.

"Sammie, there's something we've got to do," I said. "My dad told me. If we do it, we might get away with this."

I told her what my dad had said earlier that night. She gawped at me and shrugged when I was done.

We got out of the car and opened the boot. We laid every one of the briefcases on the grass verge and one by one opened them.

"It's… it's incredible," said Sammie, staring at the shimmering souls, each one alive, shining. The light from them made everything around us brighter.

"Step back," I said and eased her away. "Okay, let's hope this works."

"What are we doing?"

"We're making an offering."

"An offering?"

I looked up to the sky and then back down at the souls. They seemed to be glowing stronger. The liquid bubbled in the spheres.

"Yeah," I said, "an offering. I'm offering them to the other side. And I'm hoping they'll take them."

"The other side?"

I pointed skywards.

"Oh," she said.

CHAPTER 31.
CHASED AGAIN.

WE piled the souls back in the boot and got going again. We were driving along the road, headed for Sandwich, when I saw in my side-mirror a tiny, fiery dot in the distance – and I knew exactly what it was.

I accelerated.

Sammie jerked. "Jimmy, why are you – "

"They're coming."

I had no idea what was coming. Maybe the chariot. Maybe the winged man. Maybe the devil. Maybe something worse.

But it wasn't a surprise that they were coming. I'd expected it.

They would not let me go. I was theirs, and the souls in the boot were theirs.

They weren't going to shrug their shoulders and say, "Sod it, let's go home."

And in a way, I wanted them to come.

I wanted vengeance for Dad and for Tyler.

And I knew exactly how I was going to get it, even if it meant me dying.

Have faith, that's what my dad had told me. *Have faith*.

"I'm so scared, Jimmy," she said.

"We'll be okay, but you've got to trust me, all right?"

"I don't like the sound of that."

"You've just got to."

"Okay, I do trust you."

"Whatever you see me doing, just believe in me – have faith."

"It… it sounds scary."

"It might be."

"Jimmy," she said.

"Yeah."

"I can't believe how brave you are. I mean, I always knew you were. Sort of. When you fought Jordan for me. Stuff like that. But this… what you're doing… and coming to save me like you did… you're… you're amazing."

Just in that moment I felt okay. Everything was all right. But moments are moments because they don't last. And when I glanced behind me, any happiness I felt quickly dimmed.

"Don't look back," I told her.

She did look back.

She screamed.

The winged man flew after us, his massive wings sweeping him through the air. Flanking him was an army of demons. Their wings made a thunderous noise. There had to be fifty or sixty of them. Fire spat from their bodies. Their red eyes fixed on me. The moonlight glimmered off their brown, oily skins.

The Ford Galaxy was also chasing us.

An army of devils and thugs with guns.

Great, I thought.

Sammie stared straight ahead, her face tight and pale. She was trying not to think about what was following us, trying to look ahead – maybe to our future, though I doubted we had one.

I flagged, my hopes dwindling. I could just stop and give myself up. Beg them to spare Sammie. At least she would be safe. The angel had said she'd be all right if I won the race. Maybe I should

127

have accepted his bargain. They could have me and their souls if Sammie could go. My foot lifted an inch off the accelerator.

My dad's ghost appeared in the back seat.

"Don't trust them, Jimmy," he said.

Sammie ignored him. He was invisible to her.

He said, "Have faith, remember. Believe. But don't trust them. The devil wants you, son, and he'll be waiting for you. Have faith, have faith, have… "

He faded again.

Sammie was shouting, "They're right behind us, they're right behind us."

Something landed on the roof of the Merc, forcing us to swerve to the left.

The roof buckled as a heavy, powerful weight pummelled it, and pummelled it again.

A roundabout lay ahead of me.

To the left, Dover. To the right, Ramsgate. Behind me, hell.

"Hold on," I said to Sammie.

Adopting the cornering skills I learned at Buckmore Park and honed on the A2 as cops chased me, I wheeled the Merc to the left, cutting the corner, going straight across the opposite lane.

Whatever was on top of my roof flew off, and I glimpsed it in the mirror – a spinning, whirling ball of fire and wings.

I hit the A256 on the wrong lane. A car came straight for me. The driver flashed his full beam at me and slammed his horn.

Sammie shrieked.

I swerved out of its way.

The driver's face showed rage. But then it stretched into an expression of horror when it saw what I was running away from. The Galaxy behind me had to skid out of the oncoming car's way, which gave me an advantage over my human pursuers.

But the devils kept coming.

I hit the road hard, reaching 100mph.

Around me, the Kent countryside lay barren and empty. The lights of Dover shimmered in the distance. The road ahead looked busy.

It was the main route to the port.

It would be packed with lorries.

It would be twelve miles to Dover.

Twelve miles of racing against the scariest opponents I'd ever seen.

CHAPTER 32.
REPORTS OF UNUSUAL
SIGHTINGS.

I TOOK risks. I had to. I forced cars off the road. Trucks swerved in my way, trying to stop me, thinking I was a joyrider running from the cops. I shot off the road to avoid them, kicking up dirt, tearing through bushes. The tires screamed. The engine roared. The car groaned.

And the demons kept coming.

They overturned lorries. They tossed cars aside. They ripped up the road.

The noise was thunderous.

And then Sammie said, "There's a helicopter."

At first I thought it was chasing us. But it wasn't.

"It's really low," said Sammie. "They've got a camera."

TV, I thought. *We're on TV.*

The chopper followed the chase.

"Switch on the radio," I said.

Static crackled. Interference filled the airwaves. Voices came through, all of them laced with panic. Music blurted out of the scrawl.

Then finally a clear voice. A news channel. An incident in Kent. Canterbury hit by an earthquake.

"Earthquake?" said Sammie.

The news reported deaths.

The news reported destruction.

The cathedral damaged. The roads ravaged. Buildings collapsed.

"And now, reports coming in… " said the presenter.

Incidents further south. Accidents on the Dover road.

The news reported deaths.

The news reported destruction.

Lorries and cars overturned. Fires breaking out.

Reports of unusual sightings.

Soon they wouldn't be just reports. They'd be on people's TV screens once the helicopter transmitted its pictures.

The world would see me racing in stolen car, chased by demons.

"Are we on TV, you think?" said Sammie.

"I guess so."

"Oh no, my mum will see."

"Aren't you supposed to be playing with demons after midnight?"

"I'm not supposed to be playing with you."

"She never liked me, your mum."

"You can't blame her, Jimmy."

"No, I can't."

"She'd like you now."

"Would she?"

"You're brave – and crazy."

"Take more than that for your mum to like me."

"You were going to die for me – I think that would persuade her."

I overtook a car on the roundabout, taking the second exit towards Dover.

I nearly lost control. The Merc's wheels left the road for a few second.

Gritting my teeth, I held on, and the car came down, and I was in charge again, exhilaration pulsing through me.

"Is the helicopter still there?" I said.

Sammie said yes.

It comforted me that we were being watched. I felt now we weren't alone. We had witnesses. Someone who could stand up for me when it was done and say I wasn't guilty of whatever they decided to charge me with.

Behind me, the demons tore through traffic. As cars drove into them, they swiped them aside. Some drivers diverted and went straight into the bushes or crashed into the central barriers.

I heard sirens in the distance.

The radio had an interview with the home secretary.

My skin tingled.

The government were talking about me, or at least something I was involved in.

It made me uncomfortable.

I didn't want to be known for this.

The helicopter flew ahead of us and wheeled around to face us. The spotlight from the camera blinded me for a second. I swerved across the road.

I clipped a car coming the other way.

Horns blared.

Sammie shrieked.

Tires squealed.

My heart leapt.

I was losing control of the car.

I slowed down, allowing the demons to get closer.

They clawed at the back of the Merc. In the rear-view mirror, the winged man smiled at me – his smile said, "I've got you, you thief."

But then the helicopter swooped down, trying to get closer on the action.

The power of its rotors tossed the demons aside, scattering them.

I whooped.

Sammie said, "Go!"

I pulled away. The demons re-gathered. The helicopter followed me. It flew low. It was between me and my pursuers now.

The Ford Galaxy accelerated up behind me.

Flashes of light came from the side windows. And then gunfire.

"What was that?" said Sammie.

"The blokes in those cars, they're firing at the helicopter."

The pilot kept coming, staying low, getting some good footage. Gunfire barked.

The demons suddenly surged upwards.

"They're attacking the helicopter," said Sammie.

I watched in my mirrors.

The winged creatures swirled around the chopper. It looked like one of those balls of sardines you see with sharks and dolphins feeding on it.

Some demons got sliced up on the blades. But there were too many of them in the end.

The helicopter, wrapped in a ball of demons, spun out of control.

It plummeted to earth.

"It's going to crash," said Sammie.

And it would crash right behind us if I didn't speed up.

I bit my lip. I tasted blood. Everything hurt.

My foot nearly went through the floor.

How much faster could I go?

Seconds before it crashed, the demons sailed away from the helicopter.

The last thing I saw of it before it went up in a fireball was the pilot's eyes, wide and terrified.

A ball of fire lit up the night.

The blaze filled the night, fifty yards behind me.

The noise deafened me.

The car bucked.

I shouted. I felt the heat and the power of the blast.

Sammie ducked down.

Flames engulfed any vehicle close by.

But we were clear. We drove on, leaving the burning debris further and further behind.

I breathed out.

For a second I thought the fire had enveloped the demons.

But then they appeared in the darkness, a cloud of flapping monsters rising up out of the smoke and coming for me.

CHAPTER 33.
THE WHITE CLIFFS.

IT was 2.15am. I was knackered. I was hurting. I was starving and dizzy.

But I had to keep going.

I had to have faith. Faith that my offering would be enough. Faith that there was someone there listening to it. Faith that my dad had actually appeared to me and it wasn't some kind of dream. Faith that I had plenty of fuel.

We were running low.

The gauge nudged the red.

Still on the Dover Road, we were headed towards the junction with the A2.

Hell was still on our heels.

I could see the fire they left in their wake.

I could see the carnage.

More helicopters followed our progress now. Some of them were TV choppers, but the police were also up there.

Kent Police shares a helicopter with Essex Police. I recognized it now because it had followed me a few times in the past. You can't outrun the police helicopter, so you have to dump the car and leg it, hoping for the best.

You can also time when you nick a car because the Kent force only get the 'copter for a few hours every day.

The few times I'd had to ditch a car and make a run for it, I'd been lucky. I'd somehow got away from the infrared spotlights.

Now I wanted them to see me. I wanted them to follow.

I joined the A2, driving south.

"Where are we going?" said Sammie.

"Dover."

A roundabout lay ahead. To my right was a Total garage. I wished I could stop and fill up the tank. No chance. I kept driving. Late-night customers filling up stopped and stared at us. And then they screamed and ran when they saw what was coming after us.

Straight over the roundabout was Dover.

Right would take me to the cliffs.

I went round on two wheels, Sammie screaming and holding on.

The Jubilee Way, leading into the town centre, was blocked off by police cars.

I don't know why they thought I'd be headed there. Main routes into towns, I suppose. They were doing it to protect the public.

Anyway, I had no intention of taking that exit. I took the first one instead, towards St Margaret's At Cliffe. It was small village I'd visited with my Nan and Dad a few times. I didn't remember it much. Only that I'd stood on the White Cliffs of Dover and looked out across the English Channel. And that's where I wanted to get to. The cliffs. The sea.

Have faith, I told myself, *have faith*.

The roads narrowed and darkened.

I was breaking the speed limit. But I was used to it. Flying around narrow, single-lane roads at high speeds was nothing new to me. Usually it was me and Tyler and we laughed as we hurtled through the darkness, a cop on our tail sometimes.

I wasn't laughing now.

I was headed up Granville Road. We'd driven down into St Margaret's Bay and taken a right. The road took us past some nice houses. Trees lined the pavements. You could see the English Channel on the right, glistening in the moonlight.

The road tapered into a track that led up to the Bluebird Tea Rooms. A long time ago the building had been an old coast guard's station. I remember my Nan telling me about it. She sang that old song, too: *Bluebirds over the white cliffs of Dover*.

Ahead of me was a gate leading into a field. There was a National Trust sign on the gatepost saying this was a public footpath. You could walk along the cliffs. You could take a picnic. You could look at the sea. You could tell your girlfriend you loved her.

But I had no intention of taking Sammie for a romantic, 2.00am stroll along the cliffs.

I drove straight at the wooden gate.

Sammie said, "What are you doing?"

I said nothing. The car smashed through the gate. I heard something clank in the engine. The Merc bounced and jerked over the field. The vehicle was wrecked by now. And whatever was in the boot was pretty damaged too. Not much chance of Sammie and me getting out of this alive unless my plan worked.

Come on, car, I thought, *one last job for you to do*.

I felt a strange bond with the Merc. It would be the last car I ever stole. And it would also, hopefully, save my life.

I drove it so it faced the cliffs and put it into neutral.

Sammie's eyes were wide with fear.

"Jimmy what are you going to do?"

I glanced quickly the way we'd come.

The angel of death and its demons were racing up Granville Road.

I looked at Sammie and said, "You have to trust me."

She nodded but didn't look convinced.

"I'm making you a promise, and this is it – I know what I'm doing. It's a real promise. Not like the others I've made. It's real because it means it can save our lives. It can save our souls. I know what I'm doing."

137

She swallowed, looking scared.

I went on:

"I really love you, Sammie, and if I get out of this, I'm going straight. I'm going to college, train to be a mechanic, and then learn to race cars. I want to be with you Sammie. If you want to be with me."

She looked me straight in the eye, and then she lunged at me, and we kissed roughly, crying and saying how much we loved each other.

I smelled sulphur.

I pulled away from Sammie.

The sky was ablaze around us.

The demons surrounded the car.

From among them stepped the winged man.

"You've led us a merry dance, Jimmy," he said. "But now it's over. The race is lost, my boy."

"You buckled in?" I said to Sammie.

She nodded, yanking her seatbelt just to make sure.

Demons pressed their faces against the car windows on her side.

The angel continued. "You won the race, but you went back on the bargain we had."

"As if you would've kept your side."

"What makes you think I wouldn't?"

"You're from hell. Hardly gives you credibility on the trustworthiness front. You would've taken Tyler and Sammie too. Broken your promise."

"Have you never broken promises, Jimmy?"

I looked at Sammie. "All the time," I said. "But not anymore. I've made one last promise that I intend to keep."

"And what's that?"

"That I know what I'm doing."

He furrowed his brow. A look of doubt past across from the angel's face.

"I see," he said. "You didn't know what you were doing when you stole this car. Look at the state of it. Lucky my master cares little for material things. Only spiritual things. I hope you haven't damaged the cargo. Now, do you want to give them back to me, Jimmy, or shall I take them?"

"Why are they yours?"

"They're paid for. Shall I take them, Jimmy? Shall I?"

"What difference does it make if I hand them over or you just take them?"

He smiled. "None whatsoever. You're right. Why waste time. My master waits for you. He's been amused by your antics. Amused and enraged. He has a particularly gruesome eternity lined up for you, Jimmy. Not the dreadful solitude others suffer. But a truly burning hell. For you and your pretty golden bird there."

Sammie whimpered. I squeezed her hand.

I said, "That's not going to happen."

"It's not?" said the angel.

"No, it's not."

"Tell me why, young James?"

I glanced at Sammie and said, "Trust me, okay, trust me," and then I looked at the angel again and said, "Because I have faith."

I rammed the Merc into gear and floored it.

The car shot towards the cliff's edge.

Sammie shrieked and clawed at me.

The sea rushed towards me.

The edge came closer.

Everything in me was saying, *Slam the breaks, slam the breaks and swerve away.*

But I sped up.

One quick glance in the mirror showed me the terror and confusion on the angel's face.

The demon gawped at me.

The car shot over the cliff's edge, me and Sammie screaming as we sailed through the air before the car started to drop bonnet-first towards the dark waters below.

CHAPTER 34.
PRAYERS ANSWERED.

WHAT happened next is confusing, and I'm still not sure if any of it is real.

The car dipped forward.

My stomach lurched.

I screamed, gripping the steering wheel.

Sammie was going mental.

I thought I'd really messed it up.

My faith, whatever that was, had let me down.

And when the sea began to churn and open up, I thought I was done for.

The car went into a dive.

The sea parted into a dark, deep chasm.

Fire glowed deep inside it.

And then the fire funnelled upwards.

We plummeted towards the abyss.

Sammie unbuckled herself and clambered into the back, screaming, trying to claw her way out.

I was panting. Gravity dragged us down, fast.

The fire rose from the well in the sea and burst out of the chasm, rearing up to form a shape.

A shape of something horned, its arms reaching up towards us, the hands opening to clasp us tightly and drag us down to hell.

I looked into the fiery eyes, and my insides melted.

It was the devil.

Satan.

Lucifer.

Evil.

And he was claiming the souls I stole – and two extra ones he hadn't bargained for.

I screamed. The car plunged down.

The fiery fingers reached for us.

And then we stopped in mid-air.

Actually stopped as if time had stood still.

The sea was illuminated.

The devil snarled.

And we just hung there.

"J-J-Jimmy, look… look at this," said Sammie from the back seat.

I turned and was blinded by an incredible brightness.

A glowing, white shaft had shot down from the sky and wrapped thin tentacles around the car.

We were hanging by threads of light.

"What is it?" said Sammie.

I hauled myself up into the back beside her.

We stared at the light.

"Faith," I said.

I looked over my shoulder.

Below us the devil raged. He flailed his arms, hacking at the White Cliffs of Dover. The sea sucked him down again, and he was siphoned into the chasm.

The demons and the angel of death were whipped up off the cliff's edge and dragged down after him, and the Ford Galaxy followed, picked up as if it were a toy car.

Everything went into the abyss, and then the sea closed over them and after a few seconds settled again into its smooth, relentless rhythm.

I looked up once again through the back window, towards the light, towards heaven.

Slowly, the car was hoisted up.

Sammie gasped in panic.

I said nothing.

Suddenly, the car shot upwards and the air was knocked out me and I was dizzy, not knowing where I was, thinking I was falling.

The light blinded me. The glare was so powerful it seemed to be burning my brain. I flailed. Not knowing where I was or what was going on. I was trying to grab onto something, reach out for Sammie. But there was nothing there. I was plummeting, the wind whipping through my hair. But I was still blind. Panic filled me. Adrenaline coursed through my veins.

And then I could see.

The ground rushed up towards me.

I hit the earth and grunted.

Sammie landed hard right next to me.

She opened her eyes and panted.

"Are you okay?" I said.

"What happened?" she said.

I shook my head and looked up.

I only saw it for a second, maybe less than that, so I couldn't tell if it was real.

But the black Mercedes, with the souls in the boot, was drawn up by the light. And then it was gone, the dark sky closing over it.

And there was nothing.

"Did you see that?" I said.

"Yes, I did," she answered. "What happened, Jimmy?"

"The offering we made was accepted."

"What does that mean?"

I sat up and helped her up. She cuddled me. The sea was still. The night was quiet. I knew that behind me, the rest of Kent was in ruins. But it was peaceful here on the cliffs, looking across the English Channel, dark and still and quiet.

143

"My dad told me to offer the souls up to… to heaven," I said. "You remember them moving about when we opened the cases up? They were making a plea. They were begging for salvation. Their prayer was answered. I don't know, God or Jesus, or whoever, took them from the devil's grasp. Took them back, because my dad said they belonged to him, to God, in the first place. He took them back."

"And you had faith."

"Yes, I must have had faith."

She leaned into me. She was shivering.

I said, "We should go somewhere else, you know."

"Okay, anywhere."

"Anywhere?"

She looked into my eyes and smiled through her tears.

"Anywhere with you, Jimmy Chance," she said.

"Is that a promise?"

THE END.

AN EXCERPT FROM
THOMAS EMSON'S

ARIAH

ALSO AVAILABLE FROM
SNOWBOOKS

STAMPING GROUND.

IF it had been anyone other than Charlie Faultless walking down this street dressed in the Paul Smith navy blue suit, the Patrick Cox shoes, and the Yves Saint Laurent shirt and silk tie, they probably would have been mugged by now.

But Charlie Faultless wasn't just anyone. He had an air of menace – something about him that made it clear you'd be messing with the wrong fella.

The way he walked made you eye him up but stay well back.

He might *not* be tough. He might just look it. But a mugger had to make a split-second decision. And a swagger, a strut, and scary eyes that were different colours made all the difference when it came to making a choice – to mug or not to mug.

With Charlie Faultless, the right decision was to walk away and choose another victim.

Good call. Because the swagger, the strut, and the scary eyes weren't just show – he could back them up.

Faultless wasn't big. Five-nine, a hundred-and-sixty-eight pounds. Lean and sharp-edged, as if he'd been cut from flint.

But he was pit-bull tough. You kick off with him, he'd not let go till one of you wasn't moving much – and it wouldn't be him.

You could put him in an expensive suit, give him the handbook on how to behave in company, forge him into one of the best investigative journalists in the country, but Charlie Faultless still had the cold blood of a street fighter racing through his veins, the black heart of a villain beating in his breast.

And this was the place that made him. The Barrowmore Estate, E1.

It had been fifteen years. Nothing had changed. Graffiti and burned-out cars. Overgrown grass on a piece of open ground. Rusted swings and a climbing frame. Youths loitering, transmitting menace. The smell of booze and fags on the air. The stench of charred metal from the cindered vehicles and petrol and oil fumes from their gutted engines. The reek of dog shit from the hybrid beasts used as weapons by drug dealers. Satellite dishes festooned the tower blocks. Laundry flapped on the balconies. Snatches of arguments wheeled on the breeze.

He stopped outside a row of shops. Most of them had been boarded up. But there was a Costcutter convenience store, its windows protected by metal grilles. A burglar alarm's red light winked above the door. Bracketed to a tree outside, a CCTV camera gazed down at the pavement. Along from the Costcutter, a takeaway offered fish and chips, pizzas, and kebabs. Further down stood a greasy spoon called Ray's that offered a full English for a fiver and chips with everything.

Faultless looked around. The patch of open ground lay on the opposite side of the road. Litter was strewn in the grass. The smell of dog shit filled the air. It was obviously the place to go when your frothing, mad-eyed weapon needed a crap. Smell or no smell, it didn't put off the trio of louts swigging beer on the acre of ground. Faultless eyed them. He gripped the strap of his Gucci shoulder bag. The three wise men might just fancy it – and the MacBook tucked inside.

You ain't having it, thought Faultless. *No one's having it.*

Not even the Hodder & Stoughton publishing exec Faultless and his agent just had a curry with in Brick Lane. If they wanted the MacBook, or, more specifically, the proposal it contained, they'd have to better the offer made by Macmillan.

Faultless turned away from the three youths and looked up the road.

The sight made him shiver.

You're jumpy tonight, Charlie boy, he told himself. But he knew why.

The four tower blocks glimmered against the dark sky. They were each fifteen-storeys. Fifteen floors of misery. They were built in a quadrangle, the centrepiece of Barrowmore. They were named Swanson House, Monsell House, Bradford House, and Monro House. Surrounding the tower blocks were more flats. Rows and rows of two-storey, red-brick, pre-fab housing, raved about in the 1960s, railed against in the 2010s. Streets of these bland, clinical boxes – hailed as modern and stylish when they replaced the slums – snaked around the estate. The buildings were now damp and filthy. They were as soiled as the tower blocks looming over them, as grim as the warehouses lining the estate's forgotten corners.

Staring up at the towers, Faultless thought about the regeneration projects that had redeveloped much of the East End. Money poured in. The tower blocks were demolished and replaced by low-rise housing. Cool Britannia swooped – artists, musicians, actors. Galleries opened. A busy, lively nightlife evolved.

It was bright, it was buzzing – it was a grand illusion.

Because if you wave a magic wand, your sleight of hand will never hide every secret.

Some places you'll miss. Some secrets will stay hidden. Secrets like the Barrowmore Estate.

Faultless cringed. He nearly turned his back on the tower blocks and walked away – headed up the road that led back to Brick Lane and Commercial Street, back to civilization and sanity.

But he steeled himself. He had to do this. He had to cleanse his soul. He needed closure. He needed answers. He needed to repent.

"Hello, chief," said a voice behind him.

He wheeled, ready to kick off, fizzing with tension. This was his old stamping ground, but he'd not been back since 1996 – not since he'd been forced out. But time wouldn't have healed the wounds he'd opened. It had probably made them fester.

And there was a good chance the Graveneys would still be out for his blood.

"Twitchy, ain't you, chief," said the voice, from behind a veil of smoke.

THREE WISE MEN.

THE cigar smoke cleared and showed an old man with snow-white hair that reached down over his shoulders. His raven-black eyes sparkled as he smiled at Faultless. He scratched the tuft of beard on his chin and said, "This kind of place makes a fella twitchy, I guess. You agree with me, chief?"

Faultless narrowed his eyes, studying the man. His face was speckled with the signs of age. He wore a leather waistcoat. Tattoos swathed his arms and his torso. Faultless stared at the images and lost himself in them as they appeared to move on the old man's body.

He snapped out of it, feeling himself flush. He furrowed his brow and searched his memory, because the old man's face seemed familiar.

"You all right there, chief?" said the stranger.

"Yeah, top notch. Do I know you?"

"Might do."

Faultless thought about introducing himself, but he hesitated. Bad blood made him think twice.

He asked, "You lived here long?"

"Not round here, no. Elsewhere, though. Very long."

"Moving up in the world, are you? To Barrowmore?"

The old man said, "Up, yeah, that's right. Way up. A long way. You ain't got a couple of quid for a can to go with my cigar, have you, chief?"

"Spent all your pension on the Havana, mate?" said Faultless, still trawling his mind for a match of the old man's face.

"No, I killed a man for it."

"Well, if you need a smoke, you need a smoke…"

The old man chortled. "That's right, chief. Now, have you got a couple of quid for a pensioner to have a night-cap?"

Faultless gave him some cash. The old man winked at him and went into the Costcutter. Charlie shook his head, tutting at his own gullibility and dismissing the feeling that he'd seen the elderly man before.

Mind playing tricks, he thought. *Stress of being back.*

He turned to walk away but stopped in his tracks, the three wise men blocking his path.

Not men really – they looked about sixteen.

The betting was they weren't very wise, either.

"What you got in the satchel, mate?" said one of the boys. He was your generic yob – pasty-faced, hooded-top, a swastika tattooed on the back of his hand.

Faultless glared at the youth, and the boy faltered.

"Here," the lout said, "you got one brown eye, one blue eye. You a freak or something?"

"I'm a freak, son," he said. "You know how much of a freak?"

"You what?" said the youth as one of his mates – maybe wise after all – was saying, "Leave it, Paul. He looks weird."

The third lout was already drifting off. He was tall. Well over six-five, but piss-thin. He reminded Faultless of that old toy, Stretch Armstrong.

Faultless, fixing on the first youth, the troublemaker, said, "You take advice, Paul? Is that your name? Paul? Take your mate's advice and leave it."

But he knew he was wasting his time. Still cocky, the lad called Paul said, "What're you going to do if I don't, fucker with your suit on?"

Faultless gave him a long, hard look that appeared to make the youth's knees buckle. Then he lifted the Gucci bag and said, "You know what I've got in here?"

"No, but I'm having it," Paul answered, not backing down.

"You think so? Tell you what's inside. It's your mother. Your fucking mother. Her fucking head right in this fucking bag." The lad's eyes were widening, his jaw dropping. "And if you don't fuck off," Faultless continued, "I'll rip your fucking skull off too, and stuff it in here so you're mouth to mouth with fucking mummy dearest, her cold, dead lips on yours. See what I'm saying, Paul?"

Paul saw. He looked Faultless up and down. He backed off, still staring, still not entirely sold on the retreat option.

"Come on, Paul. We'll get him later if he's around," said the lad's mate. "Let's go find the fucking cunt who nicked the PS3."

They legged it, Paul giving Faultless the finger before he and his buddies scarpered down an alley next to the wasteground.

"Should bring back the lash. What do you say, chief?" Faultless turned. It was the old man, swigging from a can of Carlsberg. "Time we make 'em pay for their indiscretions, eh?"

"They wouldn't be the only ones paying," Faultless said. He stared at the old man, certain he'd seen him before.

He would've bet his life on it.

SETTLING IN.

HOME. At least for the next few months. A one-bedroom hovel on the tenth floor of Swanson House. The letting agent had promised great views of London and accessibility to all local amenities. Bollocks. You could see the city sprawling east towards Barking and Dagenham – lovely – and you had Costcutter with its metal grilles and CCTV, the culinary delights of the kebab shop, Ray's café, and a pub with boarded up windows. But you'd have to run the gauntlet of the three wise men – and probably a few of their mates – before you got your shopping done, picked up your supper, or had a quiet pint.

Yes, thought Faultless, studying the flat, *it's going to be perfect.*

A shit-pit. Damp darkened the walls. The paint peeling. The floorboards rotted. A musty smell hung in the air. There was a red couch, sunken and sad-looking. By a window that provided smashing vistas of far-distant estates sat a table with two chairs tucked under it.

Faultless placed his MacBook on the table. This flat would be his base while he wrote the book. He'd spend his days researching and the evenings writing. After all, there wasn't much to do around here. Lucky he had a hobby.

He unpacked the rest of his overnight gear – a change of clothes for the following day and bathroom stuff. He'd left his suitcase at his agent's office in Holborn. He wasn't going to walk into Barrowmore with it at night, telegraph the fact he'd moved in – that'd make his flat a target for yobs. Best to sneak in as quietly as possible and get his agent to send the case over tomorrow.

He ate a ready-meal spaghetti bolognese, heated in the dusty microwave. The floor of the kitchen was covered in mouse droppings. He studied them as he ate standing up, wondering if he should get a cat.

With everything done – unpacking, eating, washing – he sat at the table in front of his computer and thought things through.

The noise of the estate drifted up ten floors. It was muffled, but he could still hear it. Wheels screeching. Girls screaming. Boys laughing. Hip-hop throbbing. Babies wailing. Footsteps pounding. Dads leaving. Mothers crying. A cacophony compressed into a tiny ball of noise that was being constantly tossed at his window and his front door.

Good to be home, he thought. *Good to know nothing's changed.*

He took his notebook out, laid it on the table, and opened it to the first page. Her photo stared out at him, and he saw red. He always did. The fiery rage erupting. In the past, he would've burned someone with it – doled out a hiding, a stare enough to provoke him. Now, most of the time, he could master the fury.

He looked into her eyes and breathed, clenching his jaw, bunching his fists, letting the anger seep out of him.

It was a colour photo, taken when she was sitting at the kitchen table. He remembered taking it. The camera had been nicked. Some tourists had lost their way and decided to photograph the tower blocks, only for a seventeen-year-old Charlie Faultless to swagger over and say, "Take a shot of me, mate," the tourist mumbling, "Heh?" and furrowing his brow – and seeing the camera snatched from his grasp. Faultless swaggered off, the tourist and his wife shouting at him. When he got home, she'd been sitting at the kitchen table, smoking.

"Over here," he'd said, and she'd turned and flashed a smile saying, "No, Charlie, I look a right mess, darlin'."

"You look gorgeous, Mum," he'd said.

She did – long, dark red hair, mahogany eyes, and a face that had once appeared on the front of a teen-mag. That had been when she was a kid – just fifteen. A photographer spotted her at Oxford Circus with her mates. He'd handed her a card, told her to come to his studio. "Get your mum's permission." She said she would but never did. Her mum was a drunk who nicked the money her daughter made working weekends at Ray's greasy spoon.

So she'd gone to this photographer's studio with a mate.

"This is my mum."

"Looks young, your mum."

"Yeah, I was a kid," her mate said, grinning. "You know – modern Britain and all that."

The photos were taken. She got paid. Well, her "mum" got the cheque. A month later her picture was on the cover of the magazine, and the photographer said: "You're going to be a star." Three months later, she was pregnant. The star waned. Her skies darkened. Her future faded. Her boyfriend vanished. The child died.

But another came along. A little miracle. A 7lb 10oz bundle she named Charlie.

His murdered mother smiled at him from the photograph. It was how she would always be to him, and how he wanted to remember her. Smiling and beautiful. But the picture had been corrupted by another image – the police photos of her mutilated body.

As Charlie stared at the photo, both images mingled – the

swishing hair, the glance over the shoulder, the cigarette, the half-smile, the open throat, the cleaved abdomen, the cavernous belly, the pile of intestines…

Faultless cried out, venting his wrath.

Anger's no good, now, he thought. *This is not about vengeance.*

At least that's what he told himself, in his suit and his tie, with his middle-class manners and the cut of his dinner-party jib. That's what he told his agent. "Closure, Mike, not revenge."

Closure…

He turned the page of his notebook. Another photo, Sellotaped there, looked up at him. Rachel. Beautiful Rachel.

His heart felt as if it had shattered.

Fuck closure…